NO HARD FEELINGS

Julia Howe

dizzyemupublishing.com

DIZZY EMU PUBLISHING

1714 N McCadden Place, Hollywood, Los Angeles 90028

dizzyemupublishing.com

No Hard Feelings
Julia Howe

First published in the United States
in 2023 by Dizzy Emu Publishing

dizzyemupublishing.com

NO HARD FEELINGS

Julia Howe

NO HARD FEELINGS

Written by

Julia Howe

A Psychological thriller.

Writers Guild America West reg no: 2191357

SC 1. INT. COCKTAIL BAR. FULHAM. LONDON. DAY.

An opening **MONTAGE** with AUDIO - California Soul by Marlena
Shaw (all music suggestions are indications of what could be
used).

Our eyes are drawn to **ELLIE SOMERVILLE** [35] in a tropical-
themed bar, guzzling an enormous cocktail. She wears a pink
satin party dress and a fake garland of flowers around her
neck.

Her hair's in a dark black bob, but what you really notice
are her green eyes. She looks impish, sassy, bewitching - a
girl about town.

Next to her, and guzzling from her own glass is **SAM PENFOLD**
[36], who has a round, open, Earth-mother face and dressed
far more casually.

                    SAM:
            Don't look now, but I swear that
            guy over there is checking you out.

                    ELLIE:
            Where?

                    SAM:
            Five o'clock.

The **MONTAGE** continues: Ellie laughs flirtatiously while
chatting with various colleagues, all hip young things in
their 30's. They're standing outside the Prince of Wales
Feathers pub, London at <u>sunset</u>.

Finally: Ellie loses herself to the beat in Colours Hoxton
club in the wee small hours. We see her and Sam dancing
drunkenly together. Then she grabs a blonde, stocky guy **GRANT
WINTER**, [38] towards her using the lapels of his work jacket.

Sam is leaning against the wall, watching them, taking a
breather.

                    ELLIE:
            We really nailed it today, didn't
            we? The presentation.

                    GRANT:
                (Australian accent, from
                Sydney)
            We sure did. The old client preso -

                    ELLIE:
                (laughs)
            Preso? You're so -

                         GRANT:
              Australian?

They snog drunkenly.

Behind them, an inebriated Sam slides down the wall and bumps
onto the floor, knees bent.

                                              CUT TO:

SC 2. EXT. MANSION FLAT. FULHAM. LONDON. DAY.

On screen titles: **Two days later.**

The imposing red-brick facade of a Victorian mansion flat
block in a quiet residential street.

A hot July day, with the sun baking the tarmac on the road -
and it's still only 8 am.

The peace is broken momentarily as the front door of the
mansion flat opens. Ellie bursts out, still fastening her
earrings. The door slams shut behind her.

She looks the business and she knows it - rocking a knee-high
floaty summer's dress and high-heeled sandals.

An elderly MAN, [**MR P**, 70's] pauses at the end of Ellie's
path.

He's wearing his customary pork pie hat at a jaunty angle and
has a newspaper tucked under one elbow. With a twinkle in his
eye, he clocks Ellie speeding towards him:

                         MR P:
              Running late again?

Ellie grins at him. They go through this routine almost every
morning.

                         ELLIE:
              Not late, just not on time, Mr P.

The old man chuckles indulgently, as if it's the first time
he's heard this joke.

                                              CUT TO:

SC 3. EXT. BUS QUEUE. FULHAM ROAD. LONDON. DAY.

Ellie kicks her heels impatiently in a long bus queue, made
up primarily of smartly-dressed commuters like herself.

She swaps glances with **DAVID SWITHINS [41]**, eye-catchingly attractive in his cream shirt and tailored cotton suit. They exchange a smile. David notices that Ellie's swiping at speed through a dating app.

David edges next to Ellie.

>   DAVID:
>   You shopping for a boyfriend?

They dissolve into laughter.

>   DAVID: (CONT'D)
>   Maybe trading in your old model for
>   a newer, more improved version?

Ellie smiles shyly, pushes her fringe out of her eyes. David notices a turquoise and silver bracelet she's wearing.

>   DAVID: (CONT'D)
>   Love your bracelet. That turquoise
>   really suits you.

>   ELLIE:
>   Oh, thanks. I bought it when I was
>   travelling in New Mexico a few
>   years back -

>   DAVID:
>   No way! Whereabouts?

>   ELLIE:
>   Santa Fe -

>   DAVID:
>   I was in Albuquerque, for a
>   conference -

>   ELLIE:
>   Oh, amazing! Did you go to the
>   Turquoise Museum? I've never seen
>   so much of the stuff in my life -

David laughs.

>   DAVID:
>   Sadly, I was there for work. Barely
>   made it out of the hotel over 72
>   hours.

Ellie looks directly at him.

>   ELLIE:
>   What do you do?

>   DAVID:
>   I'm a - managing partner of my own
>   architectural practice.

David reaches into his jacket pocket, brings out his business
card.

>   DAVID: (CONT'D)
>   Bit forward of me, I know. But - .

>   ELLIE:
>   Oh, cool.

Ellie turns the card over and reads it.

>   ELLIE: (CONT'D)
>   So your office is in Farringdon.
>   But you're here in Fulham?

David smiles at her quick wit.

>   DAVID:
>   I'm sometimes in the area for work.
>   A social housing client.

Ellie smiles at this.

>   DAVID
>   Hey, umm, I don't suppose I could
>   have your number. Could I?

Ellie swiftly looks David up and down. A handsome,
professional dude with no rings on his fingers, who's clearly
in the money and with a social conscience? Big tick.

>   ELLIE:
>   Yeah, of course.

Ellie's bus draws up as she calls him from her mobile. David
glances at her number in his phone.

>   DAVID:
>   Let's keep in touch.

>   ELLIE:
>   Sure.

They smile at each other.

>   DAVID:
>   I'm taking another route in - see
>   you.

                        ELLIE:
                  (startled)
              See you.

                                              CUT TO:

SC 4. INT. DOUBLE DECKER BUS. FULHAM. LONDON. DAY.

Ellie looks down from the top deck at David. He looks up at
her, flashes her a beautiful smile.

She smiles coyly back at him.

Then David steps out of the bus queue, pushes impatiently
back through the crowd of commuters and hails a taxi.

A look of confusion crosses Ellie's face. Was he queuing just
to talk to her?

                                              CUT TO:

SC 5. EXT. OUTSIDE ZEBRA OFFICES. EUSTON ROAD. LONDON. DAY.

An establishing shot of Zebra HQ's plush advertising offices:
all steel, glass and chrome. Beautiful media types going in
and out.

                                              CUT TO:

SC 6. INT. RECEPTION. ZEBRA OFFICES. EUSTON ROAD. LONDON.
DAY.

We move past reception, more glass and chrome. Lots of gold,
silver and bronze advertising awards on display.

The bent head of **LUCY** [20's, long blonde hair] on reception
as she answers the phone.

                                              CUT TO:

SC 7. INT. ELLIE'S OFFICE. ZEBRA OFFICES. EUSTON ROAD.
LONDON. DAY.

Ellie's pounding away at her laptop in her tiny office. She
pauses for a moment, looks out at the familiar sight:
perpetual traffic crawling along the Euston Road.

On her walls: snappy quotes from creatives past and present, funky pictures from up and coming artists, and a series of pink post-it notes in a neat row with the following words:: 'Phase one', 'bus sides', 'experiential', 'OOH', 'website'.

Her Word doc is open, titled 'Chocateer 360 degree concepts' and she's three quarters of the way down the document.

Around her on the floor are screwed up pieces of paper.

Ellie's mobile beeps. A text from David: 'Dinner tonight? x D' [all texts appear as type overlaid on a transparent panel on screen].

Ellie grins, carries on typing.

                                        CUT TO:

SC 8. INT. KITCHEN. ZEBRA OFFICES. EUSTON ROAD. LONDON. DAY.

Ellie walks into the kitchen, tap, tap, tapping on her empty coffee mug with an impatient finger nail. But oh, the embarrassment, there's Grant, who she snogged the other night, fiddling around with the water filter for the coffee machine.

Ellie nearly walks out again. But Grant catches sight of her.

He gives her an awkward nod.

            GRANT:
        Hi.

            ELLIE:
        Hi.

            GRANT:
        Don't let me get in your way.

            ELLIE:
        I was just waiting for the espresso
        machine.

            GRANT:
        Ah, nearly done.

He straightens up.

            GRANT: (CONT'D)
        I'll make you one, if you like?

Ellie shrugs a 'yes'. Grant shuts up the machine, squirts inky black liquid into his cup. He takes a slurp, gags.

Ellie laughs, despite herself.

> ELLIE:
> I'll come back later.

She turns tail, walks out. Grant looks dejected.

> CUT TO:

SC 9. EXT. OUTSIDE ZEBRA OFFICES. EUSTON ROAD. LONDON. DAY/INT. BATHROOM. SAM'S HOUSE. HAMMERSMITH. LONDON.

Ellie checks her watch, it's 18.07 pm.

She dials Sam on her mobile as she walks towards the bus stop. Sam picks up.

INTERCUT BETWEEN THE TWO LOCATIONS:

> ELLIE:
> (on her mobile)
> Hey, babe. You free for a sec? I
> need your advice on a man thing.

Sam is feverishly towel-drying the family terrier, **MONTY**, in her bathroom. The scene is carnage, with water everywhere. Both Sam and Monty are soaked through.

> SAM:
> (on her mobile)
> I'm gonna start charging you for
> the number of times you've said
> that to me!

Ellie looks guilty.

> ELLIE:
> (on her mobile)
> Sorry. You know I value your
> opinion.

> SAM:
> (on her mobile)
> Somebody has to!

> ELLIE:
> (on her mobile)
> Listen, I met this lovely guy -

> SAM:
> (on her mobile)
> Not that guy from work??

                    ELLIE:
                (on her mobile)
          Grant? God, no. I got chatting to
          this dude in the bus queue this
          morning, and he's asked me out for
          dinner -

                    SAM:
                (laughing, on her mobile)
          A 'dude in the bus queue'?? What
          are you like?

                    ELLIE:
                (on her mobile)
          He approached me -

                    SAM:
                (on her mobile)
          What, he just came up to you in the
          street? That's not what we do in
          London.

Ellie laughs.

                    ELLIE:
                (on her mobile)
          No, nothing like that. He seems
          really nice.

                    SAM:
                (on her mobile)
          You could do with a nice guy after
          your charge sheet.

Ellie looks a tad crestfallen.

                    ELLIE:
                (on her mobile)
          Point taken.

                    SAM:
                (on her mobile)
          You checked him out on socials?

                    ELLIE:
                (on her mobile)
          Not yet.

                    SAM:
                (on her mobile)
          What's Aunty Sam always said to
          you?

                    ELLIE and SAM:
                    (together, on their
                    mobiles)
          'Do your research, baby!'

                                                CUT TO:

SC 10. LIVING ROOM. ELLIE'S FLAT. FULHAM. LONDON. DAY.

Ellie looks at David's socials pages. Not much personal
information on there.

Just a few recent shots of David smiling, emerging in his
swimming trunks from the surf of some exotic ocean.

Apparently he follows Real Madrid and has a passion for a
craft beer brand in Hackney.

Then she scrolls down. Ellie speed-dials Sam.

                    ELLIE:
                    (on her mobile)
          Hey babe, just looking him up -

                    SAM:
                    (VO)
          Yeah?

                    ELLIE:
                    (on her mobile)
          Can you believe it? He loves
          'Friends'??

                    SAM:
                    (VO)
          Oh, amazing!! Who's his favourite
          character?

                    ELLIE:
                    (on her mobile)
          Looks like Phoebe ...

                    SAM:
                    (VO, laughing)
          What do you know? He obviously
          likes his women quirky. Get
          yourself on that date now!

Ellie hangs up. She texts David back: 'Fab. Where? x' She
looks out of her window at the street below, smiling to
herself.

                                        CUT TO:

SC 11. INT. THE IVY RESTAURANT. CENTRAL LONDON. EVENING.

A scrubbed and elegantly dressed Ellie waits expectantly for
David. She checks her watch, then her mobile. Sighs.

A **WAITER** [male, 20's] asks if she'd like to order a drink.

                    ELLIE:
            Why not? My date's running half an
            hour late.

The waiter bows and moves off.

Ellie is half-way through a bottle of white when David
arrives, looking flushed and out of breath.

                    DAVID:
            I'm so, so sorry for keeping you
            waiting. Shareholder meeting which
            overran.

David clocks Ellie's coolness.

                    DAVID: (CONT'D)
            I hope you're not pissed off me
            with me?

Ellie shrugs.

                    ELLIE:
            It's fine.

David points at the wine bottle.

                    DAVID:
            I see you got stuck in -

                    ELLIE:
            It'd be rude not to -

They both laugh.

Smoothly, David takes charge.

                    DAVID:
            Are you ready to order?

              ELLIE:
Yeah, I was thinking of the Thai
red curry -

              DAVID:
Sounds nice. But hey, can I suggest
the caviar? Then the shepherd's pie
to follow -

              ELLIE:
OK -

The waiter appears out of nowhere. Ellie sits back as David
gives the order.

The waiter hurries off.

David grabs Ellie's hand across the table, squeezes it.

              DAVID:
I can't apologise enough about
being late on our first date -

Ellie shakes his hand.

              ELLIE:
It's fine. Don't worry about it.

But David is still holding onto her hand.

              DAVID:
As long as you're not upset with
me?

Ellie smiles. She's never met anyone so apologetic.

              ELLIE:
Not any more.

              DAVID:
Good.

David abruptly drops Ellie's hand.

                        CUT TO:

SC 12. INT. THE IVY RESTAURANT. CENTRAL LONDON. NIGHT. LATER.

As they eat, David watches Ellie closely.

              DAVID:
How's the food?

                    ELLIE:
                 (mouth full)
              Delicious.

David laughs.

                    ELLIE: (CONT'D)
              The way to my heart is through my
              stomach.

                    DAVID:
              I can see that.

Their eyes meet over the rims of their wine glasses. David
leans in closer to Ellie.

                    DAVID: (CONT'D)
              Tell me more about you. What makes
              you tick?

Ellie can feel herself glowing in the beam of David's
attention.

                    ELLIE:
              Well, I love my job. Being creative
              - but funnily enough, it's
              something I sort of fell into,
              after dropping out of drama school -

David leans in even closer.

                    DAVID:
              Was this before or after you took a
              summer job in Italy, teaching
              English?

He traces the outline of Ellie's top lip with a finger. Ellie
pulls away, surprised.

                    ELLIE:
              How do you know about that??

                    DAVID:
              You posted about it online.

                    ELLIE:
                 (Pretend coy)
              You checked me out??

                    DAVID:
              I may have had a little peek. Don't
              tell me you didn't check me out
              too?

ELLIE:
Apart from a few hunky shots of you
in your trunks, and your love of
Phoebe in 'Friends', there wasn't
much to go on.

They stop, and look at each other.

ELLIE: (CONT'D)
So what made you come up and talk
to me in a bus queue?

DAVID:
I looked at you and thought: 'Wow!
A beautiful, professional woman.
She looks like a real jet-setter.
One of a kind'.

Ellie laughs.

ELLIE:
'One of a kind'? What do you mean?

DAVID:
I dunno. There's something about
you. You know what you want. It's
very attractive -

Then David leans in and kisses her gently.

CUT TO:

SC 13. EXT. THE IVY RESTAURANT. CENTRAL LONDON. NIGHT.

Ellie and David stand, smooching, as one black cab draws up.

DAVID:
Well, that was lovely.

ELLIE:
Indeed it was.

Ellie gets in, and looks hesitantly at David.

ELLIE: (CONT'D)
Err, can I give you a lift?

David's still on the pavement. David smiles cheekily.

DAVID:
Where to?

                    ELLIE:
          Err. Home?

                    DAVID:
          Whose home? Yours or mine?

                    ELLIE:
          No, no, no. That's not what I meant
          -

David grins at Ellie's embarrassment.

                    DAVID:
          I was joking with you. I've
          actually called my own cab -

                    ELLIE:
          Ah, OK.

                    DAVID:
          I had a lovely evening, Ellie.

                    ELLIE:
          Yes, me too. Umm. See you again?

                    DAVID:
          Definitely.

As her cab pulls away, she sees David standing by the kerb,
gazing after her.

                                        CUT TO:

SC 14. INT. HALL. ELLIE'S FLAT. FULHAM. LONDON. DAY.

On screen titles: **Two days later.**

Ellie, dressed in stained t'shirt and trackie bottoms,
vacuums the rug in her hallway. The radio's on, and it's one
of the greats, Aretha Franklin.

                    ELLIE:
               (belting it out)
          R-E-S-P-E-C-T!

She pauses. The intercom to her flat is buzzing continuously.

Ellie peers at her camera, but whoever it is has their head
down.

                                        CUT TO:

SC 15. INT. COMMUNAL STAIRS. MANSION FLAT. FULHAM. LONDON.
DAY.

Ellie jogs down the stairs at full speed.

                                            CUT TO:

SC 16. FRONT DOOR. MANSION FLAT. FULHAM. LONDON. DAY.

Ellie opens the door to find David on the threshold, wearing
shorts and an expensive-looking t'shirt.

                    ELLIE:
                (amazed)
            How'd you get my address?

                    DAVID:
            And happy Saturday to you too. You
            told me when we had dinner,
            remember?

Ellie looks embarrassed, confused.

                    ELLIE:
            Ohhkay?? Did I?

David comes nearer, flirtatious. She can smell his spicy
aftershave. The whole heady, delicious combo of his proximity
and her desire is affecting her judgement, boundaries, and
all the other things you're meant to uphold when getting to
know someone you fancy.

                    DAVID:
            You said you like your food so I
            thought I'd make you an offer you
            can't refuse. Fancy a picnic in
            Hyde Park?

                    ELLIE:
            But I'm doing my Saturday morning
            clean -

David's lips are inches away from Ellie's.

                    DAVID:
            Come on, that can wait. This is way
            more fun.

Ellie lets David kiss her. Then she pulls away.

                    ELLIE:
            OK, bear with. I'll just go and get
            changed.

David grins to himself.

CUT TO:

SC 17. INT. BEDROOM. ELLIE'S FLAT. FULHAM. LONDON. DAY.

As Ellie frantically gets changed, she glimpses David through a crack in her semi-open bedroom door. He gives himself an approving glance at the long mirror in her living room.

Then she sees him study the many books on her shelves.

CUT TO:

SC 18. INT. LIVING ROOM. ELLIE'S FLAT. FULHAM. LONDON. DAY.

David whirls round as Ellie comes in, wearing a vintage A'line summer dress.

He whistles. Ellie grins.

> DAVID:
> Who's your favourite author out of all this lot?

> ELLIE:
> I'd say Virginia Woolf. Her writing really speaks to me.

> DAVID:
> I'm not surprised.

> ELLIE:
> You like her too, then?

David looks a little uncomfortable.

> DAVID:
> I mean, judging by the number of her books on your shelves.

CUT TO:

SC 19. INT. KITCHEN. ELLIE'S FLAT. FULHAM. LONDON. DAY.

David watches as Ellie grabs a drink of water, then hurriedly dumps several empty wine bottles and glasses into the sink.

> DAVID:
> The morning after the night before?

                         ELLIE:
                Something like that.

David turns to inspect the many photos on Ellie's battered
old fridge, while Ellie hurriedly washes a stained mug of
tea. On auto pilot, she dries it and puts it upside down on
her draining board.

The photos are mostly of Ellie with her arm round a series of
thirtysomething women and men, often in bars, a few showing
her bronzed on beaches or in clubs abroad.

One of the photos in the centre has heart stickers round it,
featuring Ellie with her arms round a woman with a warm
smile.

                         DAVID:
                    (points)
                Who's that?

                         ELLIE:
                My best friend, Sam. We've known
                each other since we were kids.

David nods.

                         DAVID:
                Am I right in thinking you're a
                party girl?

Ellie gives a coy smile.

                         ELLIE:
                I have been known to enjoy myself.
                But I have a serious side too.

                         DAVID:
                It's good to have a balance.

                         ELLIE:
                Glad you approve.

David points to a photo of Ellie with her arms round an older
couple in front of a hand painted sign: 'Crooked Heart Bed &
Breakfast'. The scene is rural. On one side is a meadow,
dotted with wild flowers.

                         DAVID:
                Wow, that's gorgeous. Where's that?

                         ELLIE:
                Ah, Devon. My parents moved there
                when they retired -

                    DAVID:
          They look kind.

                    ELLIE:
          Yeah, they are. I love 'em to bits.
          But they work too hard.

                    DAVID:
          I thought you said they were
          retired?

                    ELLIE:
          Exactly! Which is when they went a
          bit bonkers and opened a B&B -

                    DAVID:
          The Crooked Heart. Great name -

                    ELLIE:
          Yeah, yeah. But please, I don't
          think my poor old fridge can stand
          any more scrutiny.

David laughs.

                                        CUT TO:

SC 20. EXT. STREET. FULHAM. LONDON. DAY.

David shows Ellie to his open-top convertible.

                    DAVID:
          Your carriage awaits, mi lady.

Ellie raises her eyebrows in pleasure and surprise.

                                        CUT TO:

SC 21. INT. DAVID'S CAR. LONDON. DAY.

As David drives through London, Ellie cranes her head back at
the expensive picnic hamper sitting on the back seat. She
notices the upmarket branding.

                    ELLIE:
          That must have set you back a few
          quid -

David waves a hand dismissively.

                    DAVID:
          Ah! It's only money.

He turns and winks at her.

                    DAVID: (CONT'D)
          Always the best for my girl.

Ellie stares at David, surprised and delighted.

                    ELLIE:
          Does that mean - are you saying
          that - you want to date
          exclusively??

                    DAVID:
          Absolutely.

Ellie looks blown away.

                    ELLIE:
          Wow! Two dates, and you're in -

                    DAVID:
          When you know, you know. Right?

                    ELLIE:
          Right.

Ellie takes a deep breath, settles back into her seat,
getting used to the idea.

                                        CUT TO:

SC 22. EXT. HYDE PARK. LONDON. DAY.

MONTAGE: Ellie and David laughing and talking over their
picnic in Hyde Park.

Then David leans over Ellie, dangling a strawberry
seductively from its stem.

                    DAVID:
          Open sesame.

Obediently, Ellie opens her mouth and David pops the
strawberry in. Gazes at her steadily as she chews.

                    ELLIE:
          This is a bit intense, isn't it?

                    DAVID:
          Are you uncomfortable with
          intimacy?

                    ELLIE:
          A little, if I'm honest.

                    DAVID:
          We'll have to fix that.

He leans over, gives her a long, lingering kiss.

Later that afternoon, Ellie and David are lounging, slightly
drunk and giggly, under a tree. The sun is blazing overhead.

Ellie has a thought.

                    ELLIE:
          You know, I don't think I gave you
          my address.

David arches an eyebrow at her.

                    DAVID:
          No? How drunk were you?! Surely you
          remember that?

Ellie grimaces, ashamed. David has a point. She knows she
drinks too much.

                    ELLIE:
          No. I really don't think I gave it
          to you.

David sits upright.

                    DAVID:
          Ah, OK. Confessions time. I really
          like you, Ellie and I guess I was
          just - pretty desperate - to see
          you again. So I did something a bit
          - unorthodox - and called your
          company. Said I was a delivery
          driver with a package, got your
          address that way.

Ellie frowns, a little unnerved. Loosens her grip of David's
hand.

David notices.

                    DAVID: (CONT'D)
          Hope I haven't offended you, or
          freaked you out?

Ellie shakes her head, but her body language is still
distrustful.

                    DAVID: (CONT'D)
          I'm so sorry, Ellie. I shouldn't
          have done that. It was a bit
          creepy, I admit.

                    ELLIE:
          Damn right it was.

                    DAVID:
               (puts on a creepy voice)
          OK, hands up. I'm Creepy Guy.

Ellie bursts out laughing. David gives her one of his
megawatt smiles.

                    DAVID: (CONT'D)
          Are we good?

                    ELLIE:
          We're good.

David tickles her in the ribs and she bursts out laughing
again. Ellie tickles him back and soon the pair are rolling
around on the grass, tickling each other and hooting with
laughter.

                                             CUT TO:

SC 23. INT. BEDROOM. ELLIE'S FLAT. FULHAM. LONDON. DAY.

The pair slam against a wall, kissing voraciously, clawing
each other's clothes off. They make love.

Eventually, they fall asleep in each other's arms.

                                             CUT TO:

SC 24. INT. KITCHEN. ELLIE'S FLAT. FULHAM. LONDON. DAY

The next morning, David kisses a hung over Ellie, who is
mooching about the kitchen. He takes a swig of coffee.

                    DAVID:
          I've gotta dash. Big client meeting
          in an hour.

                    ELLIE:
          K.

David ruffles Ellie's hair affectionately.

                    DAVID:
          You're really not a morning person,
          are you?

                    ELLIE:
          I _am_ a morning person!

                    DAVID:
               (jokingly)
          You're so not. OK, how about 20
          laps round the park?

Ellie chokes on her tea.

                    DAVID: (CONT'D)
          I rest my case.

David kisses her, ruffles her hair again, and runs. She hears
her front door slam, and gives a little sigh.

She takes a large gulp of tea, empties the rest into the
sink. Then washes up her mug and places it upside down on the
draining board.

                                        CUT TO:

SC 25. INT. BEDROOM. ELLIE'S FLAT. FULHAM. LONDON. DAY/INT.
BEDROOM. SAM'S HOUSE. HAMMERSMITH. LONDON. DAY.

Ellie gazes at the clothes hanging in her wardrobe, struck by
a rare moment of indecision.

Her mobile rings, it's Sam. She picks up.

INTERCUT BETWEEN THE TWO LOCATIONS:

                    ELLIE:
               (on her mobile)
          Hi, babe.

                    SAM:
               (on her mobile)
          You sound half asleep -

                    ELLIE:
               (on her mobile)
          Well ... I had a steamy night with
          my new guy -

                    SAM:
               (on her mobile)
          Ooh, you strumpet!

                    ELLIE:
              (on her mobile)
          And I'm quite hung over.

                    SAM:
              (on her mobile)
          So how about a hair of the dog
          tonight? And then I can get to hear
          about Mr Wonderful -

Ellie brightens.

                    ELLIE:
              (on her mobile)
          I can go one better. How about I
          invite David and you around tonight
          for a meal?

Sam squeals down the phone.

                    SAM:
              (on her mobile)
          Ooh this must be serious! He's only
          just left and you're talking dinner
          plans -

                    ELLIE:
              (on her mobile)
          Well ... when you know, you know.
          Right?

                    SAM:
              (on her mobile)
          Wow, babe. I'm so happy for you.
          [beat] But I'll only come if you do
          your amazing lasagne!

                    ELLIE:
              (on her mobile)
          You're on!

                                        CUT TO:

SC 26. EXT. MANSION FLAT. FULHAM. LONDON. NIGHT.

A balmy, summer's evening.

An establishing shot of the block where Ellie lives, lights
on in multiple windows.

                                        CUT TO:

SC 27. INT. KITCHEN. ELLIE'S FLAT. FULHAM. LONDON. NIGHT.

Sam leans against the counter with her glass of red while
Ellie bobs up and down between oven and stove, tasting,
stirring, making final checks.

When she opens her fridge she discovers that the light is off
and her food is defrosting inside. She slams the door shut.

>   ELLIE:
> Fuck. The fridge has just died. And
> now my desert's melting -

>   SAM:
> Don't worry, babe, I'll put cool
> water in the sink and just dump
> everything in there.

>   ELLIE:
> Good thinking -

The buzzer goes.

                                                    CUT TO:

SC 28. INT. HALL. ELLIE'S FLAT. FULHAM. LONDON. NIGHT.

Sam wanders over, peers in at the video camera with Ellie.

>   SAM:
> There's a handsome dude with dark
> hair in a suit, carrying a bottle.
> Shall I let him in??

Ellie pushes past Sam's hair to look at the screen.

>   ELLIE:
> Yep, that's him.

>   SAM:
> Don't worry, I'll do the greetings
> if you need to check on the food.

Ellie rushes back to the kitchen.

                                                    CUT TO:

SC 29. INT. THRESHOLD LIVING ROOM/KITCHEN. ELLIE'S FLAT.
FULHAM. LONDON. NIGHT.

David walks in, looks round for Ellie.

Ellie waves at him from the kitchen. Sam approaches David.

                    SAM:
          Hi, I'm Sam, Ellie's friend.

David comes closer.

                    DAVID:
          Hi Sam, I recognise you from your
          photo.

They both smile at each other.

                    SAM:
          Ellie's told me all about how you
          charmed her in an early morning bus
          queue.

                    DAVID:
          I don't know about that. Ellie's
          told me about you. It's lovely to
          get the chance to finally meet you.

David gestures at the melting food in Sam's arms, and piles
of food bobbing around in the sink behind her.

                    DAVID: (CONT'D)
          What the hell's happening?

                    ELLIE:
          The fridge just stopped working, so
          we're trying to rescue dinner.

David laughs.

                    DAVID:
          Great timing.

                                        CUT TO:

SC 30. INT. LIVING ROOM. ELLIE'S FLAT. FULHAM. LONDON. NIGHT.

Ellie, Sam and David loll against the sofas, stuffed full.

With effort, David leans forward. Pops a final square of
feta cheese in his mouth.

                    DAVID:
          You sure can cook, Ellie.

Ellie grins.

                    ELLIE:
          You reckon?

                    DAVID:
          Y-e-a-h. Outstanding.

                    SAM:
               (With feeling)
          She's a born cook. I can just about
          burn toast. And that's it.

                    DAVID:
          I'm sure that's not the case -

                    ELLIE:
               (Laughing)
          It sort of is -

Sam is laughing her head off.

                    DAVID:
          Who does the cooking in your house
          then?

                    SAM:
          My husband, Rob. That's why I
          married him.

                    DAVID:
          Wise move. [beat] Can I use your
          little boy's room?

                    SAM:
               (points)
          Ah, it's just down the hall. On the
          right.

She watches as David makes his way across the living room.

                    SAM: (CONT'D)
               (whispers)
          OMG Ellie, he's gorgeous!

                    ELLIE:
          Yup. I know.

                    SAM:
          Seriously, he's lovely, babe.

Sam pats Ellie on the arm. Ellie turns round, grins at Sam.

                    SAM: (CONT'D)
          It's so great to see you blossoming
          again.

The friends grin at each other.

                                    CUT TO:

SC 31. INT. ELLIE'S OFFICE. ZEBRA OFFICES. EUSTON ROAD.
LONDON. DAY.

As the clock in her office says 5 pm, Ellie snaps her laptop
shut and puts on her cotton jacket.

Grant pops his head round Ellie's door.

                    GRANT:
            You on track with the Chocateer web
            copy?

                    ELLIE:
            I sent you the first draft half an
            hour ago.

Grant's caught out. He winks at her.

                    GRANT:
            Jeez, how did I miss that? Must
            have been admiring my reflection in
            the glass too much.

Ellie gives a slight laugh, Grant smiles.

A pause.

Grant's still standing there. Ellie looks at Grant
quizzically.

                    GRANT: (CONT'D)
                (nervously)
            I don't suppose you'd like to go
            for a drink - sometime, maybe?

                    ELLIE:
            Ah, sorry. In fact - I've met
            someone else.

                    GRANT:
            Right. Great. Of course.

They catch each other's eye, the sexual tension still
crackling between them.

David rings, Ellie picks up with Grant still in the room.

                    DAVID:
               (VO)
          How's about we go fridge shopping
          this evening?

                    ELLIE:
               (on her mobile)
          Funnily enough, I'm leaving work
          early to do exactly that!

                    DAVID:
               (VO)
          Great minds. Where are you planning
          on going?

                    ELLIE:
               (on her mobile)
          Errr, somewhere shitty on the high
          street?

                    DAVID:
               (VO)
          No, that won't cut it. You need
          something quality that's going to
          last. Let's meet at your office and
          I'll take you to the Kings Road,
          shopping.

                    ELLIE:
               (on her mobile)
          The Kings Road? Are you serious?
          The place where I can't afford
          anything??

                                        CUT TO:

SC 32. INT. RECEPTION. ZEBRA OFFICES. EUSTON ROAD. LONDON.
DAY.

Ellie's eyes widen as she steps out of the lift and into
reception, because there's David. Already. Lounging on a
leather chaise longue.

                    DAVID:
          Hello, gorgeous.

He rises to greet her. They kiss.

                    ELLIE:
          Wow, that was quick!!

                    DAVID:
          Don't worry, I was in the area.
          It's on my drive home.

As David ushers Ellie out, he winks at Lucy on reception.

                    DAVID: (CONT'D)
          Thanks, Lucy. Have a good night.

Lucy beams a smile back at him.

                                        CUT TO:

SC 33. EXT. EUSTON ROAD. LONDON. DAY.

Ellie turns to David, frowning slightly.

                    ELLIE:
          You seem very friendly with her?

                    DAVID:
          Suspicious soul, aren't you?

Ellie blushes.

                    ELLIE:
          Guilty as charged, I'm afraid.

David takes Ellie by the hand.

                    DAVID:
          I always make a habit of calling
          receptionists by their name.

                    ELLIE:
          Why??

                    DAVID:
          Because she's the boss.

                    ELLIE:
          Huh?

                    DAVID:
          Think about it. She knows
          everything that's going on in the
          business. One day she could end up
          calling the shots.

                    ELLIE:
          Hhm. I'd never thought about it
          like that.

Just then, Ellie's mobile beeps. She looks at it, perplexed.
She shows David an alert that says she has 'an unknown
accessory' on her phone.

>   ELLIE: (CONT'D)
>   Oh, that's weird. What does that
>   mean?

>   DAVID:
>   Oh, I get those all the time. It's
>   a mobile thing, apparently. Just
>   delete it.

Ellie obeys him.

>   CUT TO:

SC 34. INT. DEPARTMENT STORE. KINGS ROAD. LONDON. DAY.

MONTAGE of Ellie and David looking at and inside fridge
freezers. AUDIO - Get Ready by The Temptations.

Then Ellie comes to a full stop by a tall red fridge freezer.

>   ELLIE:
>   I never knew I could fall in love
>   with an electrical product. But
>   it's way outside my price range.

>   DAVID:
>   But you want it, right?

>   ELLIE:
>   Yeah. But there's no way I can
>   afford it.

David takes out his credit card.

>   DAVID:
>   Please. Let me help you.

>   ELLIE:
>   I can't take money off you.

>   DAVID:
>   My treat. Go on -

Ellie finally relents.

>   ELLIE:
>   Thank you. I'll name every ice cube
>   David in your honour.

They exchange a kiss.

CUT TO:

SC 35. INT. BEDROOM. ELLIE'S FLAT. FULHAM. LONDON. NIGHT.

Later that night Ellie and David fall into each other's arms
and onto her bed. They strip hurriedly, and embrace.

Afterwards, David strokes Ellie's hair.

>   DAVID:
>   (light)
>   Hey, I don't suppose I could get
>   some keys cut. To your flat. What
>   do you think?

Ellie looks bemused.

>   ELLIE:
>   Umm. It's a bit too soon. Isn't it?

>   DAVID:
>   Is it? We're getting on so
>   fabulously well, though. Yeah?

Ellie opens her mouth to argue.

>   ELLIE:
>   Well, yeah but -

David leans over, and kisses her.

CUT TO:

SC 36. EXT. MANSION FLAT. FULHAM. LONDON. NIGHT.

An establishing shot of Ellie's block of flats at night. The
eerie sound of foxes mating the only sound.

CUT TO:

SC 37. INT. BEDROOM. ELLIE'S FLAT. FULHAM. LONDON. NIGHT.

The sound of Ellie and David panting as they make love.

CUT TO:

SC 38. EXT. MANSION FLAT. FULHAM. LONDON. DAY.

Sunrise. Another dawn, another scorching summer's day.

                                        CUT TO:

SC 39. INT. BEDROOM. ELLIE'S FLAT. FULHAM. LONDON. DAY.

Ellie's already awake, but David is still fast asleep. She
eases out of bed, away from the dead weight of his arm around
her body.

Perches on the edge of her bed, yawns. She looks tired.

As Ellie puts on a chiffon summer blouse for work, she spies
David's mobile on her dressing table. She looks over at
David, hesitates.

Carefully, she picks up his mobile, types a couple of words
into the mobile to guess the password. It won't let her in.
Ellie tuts.

David stirs, opens one eye, catches Ellie holding his mobile.
David leaps out of bed, grabs his mobile off her.

                    DAVID:
          What the hell are you doing?

They stare at each other.

                    ELLIE:
          Sorry. I'm just cursed with being
          suspicious. Especially when it all
          seems too good to be true.

                    DAVID:
          Why??

Ellie takes a deep breath.

                    ELLIE:
          I dated this Danish guy, Karl, on
          and off for a couple of years -
          Well, basically - He cheated on me
          throughout with a work colleague.
          It gave me a big jolt. After that I
          found it really hard to trust men.

David frowns.

DAVID:
That's understandable. But for our
relationship to work, you're going
to have to learn to trust me. OK?

Chastened, Ellie nods.

Still angry, David hurls on his clothes.

DAVID: (CONT'D)
I've got to go.

He leaves without kissing her.

Shaken, Ellie sits back down slowly on the bed as she hears
the front door slam.

She goes to the window to watch him walk down the street away
from her. She sees a white van draw up outside. Two men in
overalls jump out, open the back, and between them carry a
large, tall cardboard box with pictures of an expensive-
looking fridge to the kerb.

CUT TO:

SC 40. INT. KITCHEN. ELLIE'S FLAT. FULHAM. LONDON. DAY.

With her shiny new red fridge in place, Ellie scrolls to
David, opens up their texts. There's been nothing from him
for three days now.

Ellie frowns.

She texts him a picture of the new fridge, and the caption:
'Thank you x'

CUT TO:

SC 41. EXT. SWITHINS & PARTNERS OFFICES. FARRINGDON. LONDON.
DAY.

Ellie checks her watch. It's 17.49 pm. Her expression is
serious, determined.

She shoots a look at the grey clad exterior of the building
in front of her in this quiet street, walks in.

CUT TO:

SC 42. INT. RECEPTION. SWITHINS & PARTNERS. FARRINGDON.
LONDON. DAY.

FEMI, the receptionist, looks up [30's, Black, very
attractive].

>   FEMI:
>   Can I help you?

>   ELLIE:
>   I'm here to see David. Ellie
>   Somerville.

Femi discretely eyes Ellie up and down.

>   FEMI:
>   Is this meeting scheduled or - ?

>   ELLIE:
>   Unscheduled.

Ellie can feel her face growing hot.

He, on the other hand, is effortlessly cool.

>   FEMI:
>   David's in a meeting currently. But
>   if you'd like to take a seat, he'll
>   be down shortly.

Ellie nods, looks around.

The reception is empty, save for a mixed-race boy [**BENNY**,
nine years old], who looks like he's sweltering in his school
uniform (white shirt, grey trousers and an impossibly thick
maroon blazer with an eagle on a crest. The words 'Dignitatis
et fortitudinis' are visible in in gold thread). He's
endlessly playing games on his mobile.

As Ellie slowly walks towards a chair, Benny raises his head.
Looks directly at Ellie.

>   BENNY SWITHINS:
>   You waiting for my Dad?

Ellie falters.

>   ELLIE:
>   (stutters)
>   Wh-what?

>   BENNY:
>   My Dad. You asked for David.

Then with a touch of pride:

                    BENNY: (CONT'D)
          He owns this company.

Ellie tries to hide her shock that David has a son.

                    ELLIE:
          Lovely.

She takes a deep breath. Tries to compose herself.

                    ELLIE: (CONT'D)
          So you doing something nice with
          your Dad this eve?

Benny pulls a face.

                    BENNY:
          He's got to take me to my parent's
          evening.

                    ELLIE:
          Can't your Mum take you?

Benny shakes his head vigorously.

                    BENNY:
          Mum teaches there so Dad always
          takes me.

Ellie pricks up her ears.

                    ELLIE:
          You live at home with Mum and Dad?

Benny gives her a pitying glance.

                    BENNY:
          Yeah, 'course. Where else am I
          going to live? I'm only nine -

Ellie lets this sink in. David's been playing her.

Abruptly, she gets up. Walks swiftly out, past Femi, head
down, engrossed in his mobile.

The lift door pings and out walks David. David clocks Benny,
who runs up to him.

                    FEMI:
          David, Ellie's here to see you -
               (looks around)
          Oh -

David looks dumbfounded.

                    BENNY:
               (points at the exit)
          She left -

                    DAVID:
          Oh, hell!
               (to Femi)
          Will you look after Benny for a
          minute?

Femi nods and David runs to the door, sees Ellie walking down
the street. Scrambles after her.

                                        CUT TO:

SC 43. EXT. STREET. FARRINGDON. LONDON. DAY.

David cups his hands round his mouth.

                    DAVID:
               (shouts)
          Ellie!

Ellie wheels round, clearly furious.

                    ELLIE:
          What's going on, David??

It's now David's turn to be on the back foot.

                    DAVID:
          I'm so sorry. I was looking for the
          right time to tell you -

                    ELLIE:
          Tell me, what, that you're married!
          You took me for an idiot and
          basically used me for sex -

                    DAVID:
          No! It wasn't like that. Nathalie
          and I are separated but we just -
          still live in the same house -

Ellie raises an eyebrow at him.

                    ELLIE:
          You're going to have to do better
          than that, David.

Desperately, David grabs hold of Ellie's arm, hard.

                   DAVID:
I swear, it's the truth. We don't
sleep together, we have separate
bedrooms. We're in the early stages
of divorce proceedings. If I had my
way, I'd get her to pack her bags
tomorrow, but I'd need to take out
a remortgage to buy her out.

                   ELLIE:
You told me you were a millionaire,
David. On our first date.

David doesn't meet Ellie's eye.

                   DAVID:
On paper, yes, but it's more
complicated than that.

Ellie wrenches herself away.

                   ELLIE:
You know what? Forget it. I'm outa
here.

David knows he's lost this particular battle. He watches her
walk away, a bereft expression on his face.

                                    CUT TO:

SC 44. INT. DOUBLE DECKER BUS. FARRINGDON. LONDON. DAY.

Ellie leans her face against the window. She looks shattered.
Closes her eyes. A solitary tear runs down her cheek.

                                    CUT TO:

SC 45. INT. DINING ROOM. SAM & ROB'S HOUSE. HAMMERSMITH.
LONDON. DAY.

Ellie morosely picks at her vegetables. Sam notices.

ROB PENFOLD [32, glasses, dark grizzled hair, unassuming]
carries some dirty dishes back to the kitchen.

                   SAM:
              (whispers)
How are you doing?

Ellie raises her face to Sam. She looks close to tears.

                    ELLIE:
          Gutted. Me and my terrible taste in
          men.

Sam puts her hand on Ellie's arm.

                    SAM:
          Don't beat yourself up. He's
          absolutely not worth your time,
          babe.

Rob comes in, bearing a bowl of apple crumble.

Ellie and Sam spring apart guiltily.

                    SAM: (CONT'D)
          That looks lovely, darling.

                    ROB:
          Who's not worth whose time?

Ellie rolls her eyes, downs her glass of red.

                    SAM:
          A guy called David that Ellie has
          been seeing. Turns out he has an
          estranged wife and kid rattling
          around in a house somewhere. On the
          brink of divorce, he said.

Sam takes a swig from her wine glass.

                    SAM: (CONT'D)
          Maybe it's best if you give him the
          boot. He sounds like an idiot.

Rob leans forward.

                    ROB:
          I think you should give him the
          benefit of the doubt. Divorce is a
          pretty expensive business, you
          know.

Sam raises an eyebrow at her beloved.

                    SAM:
          You've never been divorced. How on
          earth would you know??

                    ROB:
          Remember Marcus, my best mate - ?

                    SAM:
          From school, yeah -

                    ROB:
          Last year he got divorced from
          Mandy because she went and 'found
          herself' with that tantric yoga
          teacher. Ulysses.

Ellie and Sam exchange glances, but Rob is deadly serious.

                    ROB: (CONT'D)
          She got to keep the three bed semi
          in Kingston. Meanwhile, he's in a
          leaky caravan on Hackney Marshes.

                    SAM:
          That doesn't sound fair.

Sam turns to Ellie.

                    SAM: (CONT'D)
          Maybe find out a bit more about his
          home life before jumping to
          conclusions.

                                                  CUT TO:

SC 46. INT. ELLIE'S OFFICE. ZEBRA OFFICES. EUSTON ROAD.
LONDON. DAY.

Ellie's hunched over her laptop but she's not doing any work.
She's staring at the website of an upmarket private school in
Chiswick, St Alfred's. It has the eagle crest and the motto,
'Dignity and Courage'.

She scans down the list of teachers. There's a 'Nathalie
Swithins, Head of French'. Ellie clicks on the name and is
taken to a page with a head-shot of **NATHALIE SWITHINS** [35], a
beautiful, confident-looking Black woman.

Ellie reads: 'Nathalie lives in West London with her husband
and enjoys cheering her son on at football.'

                                                  CUT TO:

SC 47. EXT. TUBE STATION. FARRINGDON. LONDON. DAY.

That evening, Ellie walks out of the tube and heads along the
street.

She looks focused.

                                                    CUT TO:

SC 48. EXT. OPPOSITE SWITHINS & PARTNERS OFFICES. FARRINGDON.
LONDON. DAY.

Ellie waits, leaning against a tree diagonally opposite
David's practice.

Ellie puts in her headphones. AUDIO: Blame by Gabriels.

David steps out of his office, on his mobile. Ellie checks
her watch: 18.24 pm.

David walks down a cul de sac, still on his mobile. Towards
his car. Unlocks it, climbs inside.

Ellie hails a black cab.

                                                    CUT TO:

SC 49. INT. BLACK TAXI. FARRINGDON. LONDON. DAY.

Ellie leans forward in her seat.

                    ELLIE:
                 (points)
            Follow that car, please.

                                                    CUT TO:

SC 50. EXT/INT. BLACK TAXI. LONDON. DAY.

Ellie leans back and watches as London's streets fall away
outside the window. She looks lost, a little sad.

They cross London as summer rain falls.

                                                    CUT TO:

SC 51. EXT. CUL DE SAC. CHISWICK. LONDON. DAY.

David's car turns into a quiet, suburban cul de sac with
period properties at a polite distance from each other.

Ellie gets out of the cab round the corner, and goes to stand
behind tall poplar trees in a small copse within eye line of
his house.

She watches as Nathalie unloads a smaller car parked in the driveway.

Nathalie hoists several shopping bags out of the boot of her car. Benny is still sitting in the back.

From Ellie's vantage point, she sees David help Nathalie carry the heaviest shopping bags. Nathalie stumbles over a stone on the drive.

David instantly puts his hand protectively on her lower back to steady her. It's an intimate gesture, and Ellie frowns. They walk to the front door together, and then wait for Benny to get out of her car.

Ellie marches across the road angrily towards them. David is bent over Benny, who is sat on the front door step, checking scuff marks on his white trainers. Benny notices Ellie first. He grins.

>   BENNY:
>   It's the lady from the office!

David looks up. Ellie is standing in front of him, looking upset.

>   ELLIE:
>   Hey!

She gives him an angry stare.

David straightens up, shocked to see her.

>   DAVID:
>   Hi??!!

Nathalie turns round, stares at Ellie.

Ellie walks up to Nathalie, shakes her hand.

>   ELLIE:
>   Are you Nathalie, David's wife?

David turns to Benny.

>   DAVID:
>   Inside. Now!

Benny runs indoors.

>   NATHALIE:
>   (French accent, from
>   Paris)
>   Yes. Who are you??

                    ELLIE:
          Ah, he hasn't told you about me,
          has he? How sweet. I'm Ellie,
          David's lover. I'm just carrying
          out some background checks. Trying
          to divide the bullshit from
          reality, as I don't believe a word
          he's told me about his home life.

Nathalie starts visibly shaking. David squares up to Ellie,
furious.

                    DAVID:
          You have no right coming here.

                    NATHALIE:
               (fearful)
          What did he tell you?

Ellie can't help herself.

                    ELLIE:
          He said you were separated, had
          separate bedrooms. On the brink of
          divorce.

Nathalie puts her hand to her head, as if to shield herself
from a blow.

                    NATHALIE:
          Oh, Mon Dieu.

She bursts into tears.

                    DAVID:
          Don't listen to her, Nathalie.
          She's a fantasist, some girl I met
          in a bus queue once and she's been
          harassing me ever since -

Now it's Ellie's turn to be riled.

                    ELLIE:
          Don't you dare!! You swear undying
          love to me every time we sleep
          together. Maybe I'm not even the
          first?

A flicker of embarrassment and shame crosses David's face.

He darts a look at an upstairs window, where a lamp has been
switched on, and Benny is stood next to it, looking glumly
down at them all.

Nathalie sits down heavily on the front step.

>   DAVID:
>   (under his breath to
>   Ellie)
>   We can't do this here.

>   ELLIE:
>   Why not here?? Let's have it all
>   out in the open. You'd love that,
>   wouldn't you??

For the first time in their exchange, David looks Ellie
squarely in the eye.

>   DAVID:
>   Carry on involving me and my family
>   in your weird little psychodrama
>   outside my property, and I <u>will</u>
>   report you.

Ellie gives a sarcastic laugh.

>   ELLIE:
>   You wouldn't dare.

But David's face is set.

>   DAVID:
>   You've done enough damage, Ellie.
>   Go.

Ellie turns on her heel and walks away from them, vengeful,
furious, and even a little triumphant.

>   CUT TO:

SC 52. EXT. CHISWICK HIGH ROAD. CHISWICK. LONDON. DAY.

Yet surrounded by people going about their business, the
reality of what she's just learnt hits Ellie.

She bursts into tears.

People stare, but nobody intervenes.

>   CUT TO:

SC 53. INT. BEDROOM. ELLIE'S FLAT. FULHAM. LONDON. DAY.

Ellie hurls herself face down on her bed, sobbing.

Her mobile pings. A text from David. It says: 'So sorry, I can explain. Can we talk? XX D'.

Ellie curls up into a ball, consumed by misery.

Then finally she reaches a decision, and sends David a text: 'No hard feelings, but we're over. Don't ever contact me again.'

She switches off her mobile and lies motionless, staring at a picture of her and David blue tacked to her wall.

                                                    CUT TO:

SC 54. EXT. MANSION FLAT. FULHAM. LONDON. NIGHT.

A time lapse view of the block of flats as the sky fades to pink, to velvet, and then with ribbons of apricot sunrise.

                                                    CUT TO:

SC 55. INT. RECEPTION. ZEBRA HQ. EUSTON ROAD. LONDON. DAY.

Wearily, Ellie walks into work reception.

                    LUCY ON RECEPTION:
          You look tired, babe.

                    ELLIE:
          Yep.

                                                    CUT TO:

SC 56. INT. LIFT. ZEBRA HQ. EUSTON ROAD. LONDON. DAY.

Ellie props herself up against one of the lift walls. Her mobile beeps with a text from David.

Ellie reads it: 'Guess what! Nathalie's chucked me out of the house so I'm a free man. Let's make a go of it XX.'

Puts her mobile back in her pocket, her face grim.

                                                    CUT TO:

SC 57. INT. LIVING ROOM. ELLIE'S FLAT. FULHAM. LONDON. NIGHT.

Ellie slumps on her sofa, knocks back a glass of red. She looks tired and sad.

Her mobile rings, it's David. Ellie hesitates, then picks up.

David's crying. Ellie straightens up. She's never heard him like this before.

> DAVID:
> (VO)
> I'm gutted, Ellie -

> ELLIE:
> (on her mobile)
> Sorry.

> DAVID:
> (VO)
> What really upsets me is you
> thought that I - lied about
> Nathalie and me no longer being
> together -

> ELLIE:
> (on her mobile)
> But you did, David. You did lie. Or
> at the very least, you should have
> told me you still lived together.

> DAVID:
> (VO)
> Can't we just meet and talk things
> over? It's easier face to face.

Ellie's silent.

> DAVID: (CONT'D)
> (VO)
> You know, Nathalie and I - we
> married way too young. We were just
> - two lonely souls lost in London
> who met in a scuzzy bar. Our
> marriage was a sham pretty much
> from day one. That's the honest
> truth.

> ELLIE:
> (on her mobile)
> I'm so sorry, David. But I don't
> trust you anymore.

> DAVID:
> (VO, panicked)
> But - pls- I'm not like Karl!

Ellie reacts as if she's been shot.

                    ELLIE:
                (on her mobile)
              Goodbye, David.

She hangs up, switches off her mobile.

Slumps back against the sofa.

After a while, Ellie's eyes close. She gives a twitch, falls
asleep.

                                        CUT TO:

SC 58. INT. LIVING ROOM. ELLIE'S FLAT. FULHAM. LONDON. DAY.

Morning sunshine streams in. Ellie wakes, stiff and bleary-
eyed, on the sofa.

Switches on her mobile. 27 texts overnight from David, four
missed calls, one voice mail.

                    ELLIE:
              Ugh, no.

She deletes the voice mail without listening to it.

A cold cup of tea is on the coffee table. Ellie frowns.

                                        CUT TO:

SC 59. INT. RECEPTION. ZEBRA HQ. EUSTON ROAD. LONDON. DAY.

Ellie walks into reception, nods at Lucy. A huge, expensive-
looking bouquet of sunflowers is on the reception desk.

                    LUCY ON RECEPTION:
              These are for you -

                    ELLIE:
              Oh. Really?

She takes up the bouquet. Frowns. She recognises David's
handwriting on the note.

                    ELLIE: (CONT'D)
              I don't think so.

                    LUCY ON RECEPTION:
              And David's waiting over there -

Ellie whirls round. David is sitting in reception, watching
her.

Ellie rams the flowers in the nearest bin, and marches off
into the lift.

Lucy stares at her open-mouthed. Shrugs at David, who shakes
his head.

                                              CUT TO:

SC 60. INT. KITCHEN. ELLIE'S FLAT. FULHAM. LONDON. NIGHT.

Ellie comes in, still in her work clothes. She notices one of
her sash windows is slightly open, and hurries to shut it.

                    ELLIE:
                (to herself)
            God, it's freezing. Where are the
            keys?

She sighs, roots around in a china bowl full of coins, rubber
bands - but no sash window lock keys.

                    ELLIE: (CONT'D)
                (to herself)
            Where are they - ? I'm sure I put
            them -

She turns round and walks out again.

                                              CUT TO:

SC 61. INT. BEDROOM. ELLIE'S FLAT. FULHAM. LONDON. NIGHT.

Ellie sits, knees to chest, on her bed. Her mobile beeps with
a text from David.

Ellie heaves a sigh, picks up her phone. His message reads:
'Sorry to inconvenience you. You won't hear from me again.'

Ellie breathes out with relief.

                                              CUT TO:

SC 62. INT. RECEPTION. ZEBRA HQ. EUSTON ROAD. LONDON. DAY.

Ellie walks in, only to be greeted by Lucy, looking a little
under pressure.

                    LUCY ON RECEPTION:
               David and his team arrived ten
               minutes ago, said something about
               you pitching to them for some new
               business? They're waiting in
               Conference room two -

Ellie's eyes widen in horror. She hurries off.

                                          CUT TO:

SC 63. INT. CONFERENCE ROOM TWO. ZEBRA HQ. EUSTON ROAD.
LONDON. DAY.

The swankier of Zebra's meeting rooms is encased in glass.

David rises to greet her as if nothing has happened. He
introduces her to his business partner, **LORETTA TINDALL**
[40s], a sulky-looking woman with auburn hair in a black silk
shirt and dark trouser suit, and **JIM MOID**, [50's] bald and
sunburnt, MD of Penstamen Homes.

                    DAVID:
               Have you read the briefing
               documents I sent over at the start
               of the week? Had a chance to
               collect your thoughts?

Ellie looks terrified. David gives a small smile.

                    ELLIE:
               What briefing documents?

                    DAVID:
               I sent them over Sunday night.
               Everything was explained clearly in
               my voice mail.

                    ELLIE:
                 (voice quavering)
               I haven't yet got to the documents
               in my email.

David doesn't blink.

                    DAVID:
               Sorry, is this a bad time?

                    ELLIE:
               Perhaps we can reschedule when I've
               had a chance to digest the
               documents and come back with my
               response?

David confers with his colleagues.

> DAVID:
> We'll let you know.

They stand.

Loretta directs a pitying look in Ellie's direction as she sweeps out of the room, and Jim gives her an awkward nod.

When they're alone:

> ELLIE:
> (hisses)
> What the hell are you playing at? I was completely unprepared!

CUT TO:

SC 64. INT. CORRIDOR. ZEBRA HQ. EUSTON ROAD. LONDON. DAY.

Grant, walking past the meeting room, does a double-take at Ellie's fierce, intimate posture with David.

CUT TO:

SC 65. INT. CONFERENCE ROOM TWO. ZEBRA HQ. EUSTON ROAD. LONDON. DAY.

The stand-off continues between Ellie and David.

> DAVID:
> Look, it was the only way I could get to see you -

> ELLIE:
> You saw me the other day when you brought those ridiculous flowers in! This is starting to be seriously creepy, David.

David's expression hardens. He takes a step back.

> DAVID:
> OK. From now on, let's keep this professional, shall we?

> ELLIE:
> Fine by me.

David starts to walk away, stops and turns to Ellie:

                    DAVID
          Though I could say your behaviour
          reflects poorly on your tin pot
          little company, and you've probably
          blown your chances with my guys.
          Jim doesn't like to fuck about.

                    ELLIE:
          Neither do I.

David walks out.

Ellie is left seething, clenching her hands over and over.

                                        CUT TO:

SC 66. INT. LIVING ROOM. ELLIE'S FLAT. FULHAM. LONODN. NIGHT.

MONTAGE: Ellie swigging from a bottle of red. Then she
furiously texts David: 'Don't ever surprise me again, you
absolute piece of shit!'

Pours herself another glass, and then knocks it over as she
stands up from the sofa. The glass smashes and red wine
trickles onto the floor. Ellie texts David again. And again.

Hurls her mobile against the wall. Slumps back down on the
sofa, drunk. Falls asleep.

Her mobile constantly flashes and beeps with texts from
David, the blue light making eerie shadows on the wall.

                                        CUT TO:

SC 67. INT. LIVING ROOM. ELLIE'S FLAT. FULHAM. LONDON. DAY.

Another dawn, another hangover. Ellie opens her eyes. She
looks grey.

She picks up her mobile and her face freezes with horror as
she looks at the drunken, abusive texts she sent David last
night: 'For all the hurt and pain you've caused me I
sincerely hope you get hit by a fucking bus - '

                    ELLIE:
               (under her breath)
          Shiiiit -

                                        CUT TO:

SC 68. INT. MABEL'S TAVERN. EUSTON. LONDON. DAY.

Ellie and Grant are having a working lunch of fish and chips.

Ellie looks pale and strained. Her customary bounce and poise
seemingly gone.

                    GRANT:
          How's the grub?

                    ELLIE:
          Good.

Grant wipes his mouth with his napkin, places his elbows on
the table. Looks carefully at Ellie.

                    GRANT:
          Look, I don't wanna put your nose
          out of joint. I don't really know
          how to put this but -

                    ELLIE:
          What? Spit it out.

                    GRANT:
          See, the thing is - The quality of
          your output has dipped over the
          last couple of weeks. I just want
          to know: is something going on that
          I need to be aware of?

Ellie flushes.

                    ELLIE:
          What in particular do you think's
          been affected?

                    GRANT:
          Well, I'm not the best judge, but -

Glancing around, Ellie sees David seated a few tables away,
watching her avidly.

She freezes. Grant notices.

                    GRANT: (CONT'D)
          Wassup?

                    ELLIE:
               (under her breath)
          Remember that guy I told you about,
          David, the one I was seeing?

                    GRANT:
          Yeah?

                    ELLIE:
          I ditched him last weekend and he's
          sitting over there.

Grant gives David a swift look.

                    GRANT:
          Ouch.

                    ELLIE:
          A few days after I finished with
          him, he organised an impromptu
          pitch meeting with his team at the
          agency.

Grant stares at Ellie, aghast.

                    GRANT:
          So he was the 'client' you were
          having that meeting with? It all
          seemed a bit tense.

                    ELLIE:
          Yeah. He told me he did it because
          was desperate to see me.

                    GRANT:
          Oh, God.

                    ELLIE:
          I was planning to tell you - but I
          was too embarrassed. I don't want
          to be dramatic, but he's starting
          to freak me out -

Grant rises from the table.

                    GRANT:
          Oh, no. We can't have some dickhead
          hassling my star copywriter -

                    ELLIE:
          No Grant, please don't -

Too late.

Grant strides over to where David is sitting, nursing a pot
of tea.

David looks up.

                    DAVID:
          Can I help you?

                    GRANT:
          Yeah, on behalf of Ellie
          Somerville, please fuck off and
          leave her alone!

David smirks.

                    DAVID:
          You feeling alright, pal? How's the
          liquid lunch?

People at tables nearby turn and stare.

                    GRANT:
               (softly, to David)
          Leave her alone. Understand?

David nods mutely. Grant returns to Ellie.

                    ELLIE:
          Grant, let's go.

Ellie takes Grant's arm, steers him out of the pub.

                                        CUT TO:

SC 69. EXT. OUTSIDE MABEL'S TAVERN. EUSTON. LONDON. DAY.

On the pavement outside, Ellie rounds on Grant.

                    ELLIE:
          You shouldn't have done that.

                    GRANT:
          I'm not going to stand by and watch
          you suffer, and your work go down
          the toilet. Because of some prick.

They return to the agency in silence.

                                        CUT TO:

SC 70. INT. SUPERMARKET. TOTTENHAM COURT ROAD. LONDON.
EVENING.

Ellie wearily walks down the meat aisle, swings some lamb
chops in her basket. Suddenly, she turns on a whim. She feels
that someone is watching her.

She scans the other shoppers pushing past her or trundling their trollies round. Nobody pays her any attention.

Slowly, she walks her basket down to a till, and joins a queue.

And there, in the queue opposite her, is David. Standing there with his arms folded. Just staring at her. Like it's the most natural thing in the world.

Ellie puts her basket carefully down on the ground and then walks out of the supermarket as fast as she can. Expressionless, David watches her go.

                                        CUT TO:

SC 71. INT. ELLIE'S OFFICE. ZEBRA OFFICES. EUSTON ROAD. LONDON. DAY.

At her laptop, Ellie writes a bit, then stops. Stares into space.

Her mobile beeps with a text from David. Then another and another. A constant rhythm.

There's a knock, but before Ellie can say anything, Grant's opened the door.

                    GRANT:
            A few of us from the account team
            are going for some drinks after
            work if you'd like to join us?

Ellie smiles tightly. Shakes her head.

Grant eyes Ellie.

                    GRANT: (CONT'D)
            Forsaken drink?

Ellie nods.

                    GRANT: (CONT'D)
            Taken a vow of silence?

Ellie smiles. There's something about Grant that makes her warm to him.

                    ELLIE:
            Just not up to it at the moment.

                    GRANT:
          You're not thinking too much about
          that dickhead, are you?

                    ELLIE:
          Well, yeah.

                    GRANT:
          In that case, Dr Winter prescribes
          you some time out with the
          SnackSnack's account team to cheer
          you up. And I hear tell that Lucy
          from reception is having her
          leaving do tonight, so the plan is
          to join two soirees into one.

Ellie gives a half-laugh, half-groan.

                    GRANT: (CONT'D)
          No excuses. Get your coat.

They leave together.

                                        CUT TO:

SC 72. INT. PUB. EUSTON. LONDON. NIGHT.

A sizeable gaggle of Ellie and other colleagues are at Lucy's
leaving do/SnackSnack team drinks.

Ellie has a large glass of wine beside her. She looks
flushed, wired - and exhausted. But she's munching crisps
with work mates as if nothing's the matter. Grant's there,
next to her.

LATER:

                    GRANT:
               (jokingly)
          You read Drama at Uni, surely you
          can stretch to a bit of karaoke??
          Creatives against the Account team?

                    ELLIE:
          Oh, hell no -

                    GRANT:
          But I could see you in sequins and
          swinging from a trapeze, Ellie -

           ELLIE:
         (laughing)
Not for karaoke. Isn't that more
your look, Grant?

She looks up suddenly, on an instinct.

There's David, sitting at the other end of the bar, flirting
outrageously with Lucy. She's laughing her head off. David
utterly ignores Ellie.

          ELLIE: (CONT'D)
        (under her breath to
         Grant)
Don't make it too obvious, but
David's sitting at the end of the
bar on our left!

Grant turns to Ellie, a bit sozzled.

          GRANT:
        (whispering back)
Want me to speak to him, or punch
his lights out for you? Either way,
I don't mind.

          ELLIE:
        (whispering)
No, no. I'm going to leave.

          GRANT:
        (whispering)
Oh, no. Don't go because of him.
Stay!! He's an arsehole, just
ignore him -

          ELLIE:
        (whispering)
No, I can't. Don't cause a scene -
don't say anything to him.

Grant nods, puts a finger to his lips.

          GRANT:
'Course, babe.

Ellie pats Grant affectionately on the head, puts money on
the table, makes her excuses, and runs.

David looks up and stares after her.

                              CUT TO:

SC 73. INT. DOUBLE DECKER BUS. EUSTON. LONDON. NIGHT.

Ellie bites her nails down, one by one.

                                        CUT TO:

SC 74. INT. LIVING ROOM. ELLIE'S FLAT. FULHAM. LONDON. DAY.

Ellie hunches on her sofa in a big baggy jumper and trackie
bottoms, last night's empty wine bottle and glass on the
table in front of her. Her face is pale and puffy, hair
unwashed.

She has a video call open on her laptop. She leans forward as
her Mum's suntanned face, crowned by her white hair, leans
into frame [**CONNIE SOMERVILLE**, 70's].

                    CONNIE:
          Ah, it's so good to see you,
          darling.

                    ELLIE:
          Yes, Mum, you too.

On screen, Connie's sitting in a sun-drenched breakfast room
dotted with little tables covered in spotted plastic table
cloths.

Ellie's Dad, **PETER SOMERVILLE** [70's], wears an apron bearing
the words, 'World's Best Dad'. He hoovers incessantly in the
background. Connie turns round:

                    CONNIE:
          (shouts)
          Peter, turn that thing off, will
          you? Ellie's on the computer.

Ellie smiles, despite herself.

Her Dad bustles over and sits down next to Connie.

Ellie grins.

                    ELLIE:
          How's the Crooked Heart?

                    CONNIE:
          Good. Busy.

She turns to Peter for confirmation. Peter nods.

                    PETER:
          We've met one of your friends. A
          David somebody?

Ellie's face falls.

                    ELLIE:
          David Swithins??

                    PETER:
          That was it.

Ellie's face falls even further. She perches on the edge of
her sofa.

                    CONNIE:
          He's a very polite young man, says
          he's on a break from London for a
          few days, sightseeing for a
          possible house move down here. He
          wrote some very complimentary
          things in our visitor book. 'A home
          from home', he said.

                    ELLIE:
               (with gritted teeth)
          That's nice, Mum. Did he say
          anything else?

                    PETER SOMERVILLE:
          Why don't you ask him yourself?

Before Ellie can say anything else, Peter swings the laptop
round and - horror of horrors - there's David, grinning, at
their shoulders.

                    DAVID:
          Hi Ellie, lovely place your parents
          have here.

                    ELLIE:
          Yep. Thanks.

                    DAVID:
          You should come down here for a
          couple of days. We could spend some
          quality time together. What do you
          say, Fiancée?

                    PETER:
               (bemused, to Ellie)
          Fiancée?? First I've heard of it.

                    CONNIE:
          Oh, you never told us you were
          engaged! Spend some time together
          with us, darling -

                    ELLIE:
          Sorry, Mum, gotta go - . I'll call
          you -

Her parents look shocked and surprised as she hurriedly
leaves the call.

Ellie slams her laptop shut and sits there with her elbows on
her knees for a long time after that, staring at a picture of
her and her parents in a frame on her TV.

Her Mum calls her, but Ellie doesn't pick up.

Instead, she bursts into deep, heaving sobs.

After a while, she sits up, wipes her eyes. With everything
that's happened with David, it's time to make a decision.

She presses delete on all of David's texts on her mobile.
Erases his videos, his screen shots, eradicating every trace
of his presence.

Breathes out. She feels cleansed. Lighter.

                                        CUT TO:

SC 75. INT. CORNER SHOP. EUSTON. LONDON. NIGHT/INT. LIVING
ROOM. SAM'S HOUSE. HAMMERSMITH. LONDON. NIGHT.

Ellie trails round the corner shop. She looks exhausted.

Sam is calling her from her sofa. Ellie hesitates, then picks
up.

INTERCUT BETWEEN THE TWO LOCATIONS:

                    ELLIE:
          (on her mobile)
          Wassup, babe?

                    SAM:
          (on her mobile)
          Just checking in. [beat] You don't
          text, you don't call.

ELLIE:
(on her mobile)
I know, I'm sorry I haven't been in touch. [beat] I've just been buried in work the last few weeks, late nights. Tonight will be another long one.

SAM:
(on her mobile)
Where are you now?

ELLIE:
(on her mobile)
Oh, at the office.

SAM:
(on her mobile)
It sounds like you're out and about.

ELLIE:
(on her mobile)
Yeah, I just popped out to grab a bite to eat.

SAM:
(on her mobile)
Ah, OK. Maybe one of these days you might like some company?

ELLIE:
(on her mobile)
Aww, honey. I don't really feel like socialising much at the minute
-

SAM:
(on her mobile, hurt)
Hhm. As long as you're alright.

ELLIE:
(on her mobile)
I'll call you soon, I promise.

Ellie rings off. Then loads up ten bottles of red wine from her shopping basket onto the till conveyor belt.

CUT TO:

SC 76. EXT. STREET. FULHAM. LONDON. NIGHT.

Ellie wearily gets off her bus and walks up her road.

As she approaches her front door she sees a white van outside, and removals guys in overalls lifting her fridge back into the van.

She breaks into a run.

                    ELLIE:
               (shouts)
          Hey! What's going on?

One of the removals men turns round.

                    REMOVALS MAN:
          Sorry, love, we had a request to
          take your fridge back to the
          warehouse. It's faulty, apparently.

Ellie starts to shake.

                    ELLIE:
          It was working!! How the hell did
          you get into my flat?

                    REMOVALS MAN:
          Nothing to worry about. Your
          fiancé, David, was very helpful. He
          let us in.

                                        CUT TO:

SC 77. INT. COMMUNAL LANDING. MANSION FLAT. FULHAM. LONDON. NIGHT.

Ellie races to her front door, panting. It's open.

Very softly and carefully, she goes in.

                                        CUT TO:

SC 78. INT. ELLIE'S FLAT. FULHAM. LONDON. NIGHT.

Trembling, she walks into every room.

No sign of David.

                                        CUT TO:

SC 79. INT. KITCHEN. ELLIE'S FLAT. FULHAM. LONDON. NIGHT.

An empty space where the fridge was, and melting piles of food dumped in pools of water on the floor.

Slowly Ellie sits down at her breakfast bar. She hears the
kitchen tap dripping slowly. Ellie closes her eyes.

Suddenly, Ellie opens her eyes, jumps up.

                                                    CUT TO:

SC 80. INT. HALL. ELLIE'S FLAT. FULHAM. LONDON. NIGHT.

Ellie races down the hall, bolts her front door from inside.
Then we see her tearing round her flat, bolting windows and
drawing curtains.

                                                    CUT TO:

SC 81. INT. KITCHEN. ELLIE'S FLAT. FULHAM. LONDON. DAY.

The next morning, Ellie vacantly sips at her coffee,
surrounded by sodden bags of melted food piled high on the
sink draining board.

Grant calls Ellie's mobile. Ellie picks up.

                    GRANT:
                 (VO)
              Where are ya? We've got a client
              progress call in 15 minutes.

                    ELLIE:
                 (very quiet, on her
                  mobile)
              Sorry. Something came up and I'm
              working from home.

[PAUSE]

                    GRANT:
                 (VO)
              You're not OK, are you?

                    ELLIE:
                 (on her mobile)
              Not really.

                    GRANT:
                 (VO)
              K, let's talk about it later. I'll
              ping you a link.

                                                    CUT TO:

SC 82. INT. KITCHEN. ELLIE'S FLAT. FULHAM. LONDON. DAY.

Ellie stands at the sink, staring blankly out of the window.
She realises she's left the cold tap running. Her hands are
red and numb with cold.

A text from Grant: 'Give me your address and I'll come over.'
Ellie texts Grant her address.

                                             CUT TO:

SC 83. INT. HALL. ELLIE'S FLAT. FULHAM. LONDON. DAY.

Ellie checks her camera and then opens the front door as
Grant approaches. It looks as if he's had a shave and combed
his hair.

As Ellie shuts the door behind him, she gets a whiff of after
shave.

Grant looks expectantly at her.

                    GRANT:
          What's been occurring?

                    ELLIE:
          Let me show you.

                                             CUT TO:

SC 84. INT. KITCHEN. ELLIE'S FLAT. FULHAM. LONDON. DAY.

Grant takes in the wilting mountain of food beside the sink,
the square indentations in the lino where a fridge once
stood.

                    GRANT:
          OK, talk to me.

Ellie hesitates.

                    ELLIE:
          When we were going out together,
          David insisted on buying me a new
          fridge.

Grant raises an eyebrow.

                    ELLIE: (CONT'D)
          Yeah, I know. Now he's my ex he had
          it taken away.

                    GRANT:
          So he enjoys messing with your
          refrigeration?

Ellie stares at Grant, not sure if he's joking or not.

                    ELLIE:
          Grant, he let himself into my flat
          while I was out to let the removals
          guy take the fridge. And I swear he
          keeps moving stuff around -

Grant's expression becomes serious.

                    GRANT:
          He 'let himself' into your flat?
          How come?

                    ELLIE:
          He must have had some keys cut -
          even though I didn't give him
          permission -

                    GRANT:
          Shit, man. Let me go over there
          with a coupla mates and have it out
          with him.

                    ELLIE:
          Don't Grant, please. Beating the
          shit out of him's not going to
          solve anything.

                    GRANT:
          Right, in that case. How about we
          change the locks?

                                        CUT TO:

SC 85. INT. COMMUNAL HALL. MANSION FLAT. FULHAM. LONDON. DAY.

Ellie looks on admiringly as Grant fixes a new lock to the
front door of her flat.

                                        CUT TO:

SC 86. EXT. MANSION FLAT. FULHAM. LONDON. DAY/INT. DAVID'S
CAR. LONDON. DAY.

Grant snaps shut his box of tools.

                    ELLIE:
          Thanks so much. You're a star -

                    GRANT:
          Hey, no problem. Hopefully now
          you'll feel a bit safer.

Grant's mobile goes, Grant picks up.

                    GRANT: (CONT'D)
               (on his mobile)
          Hello?

INTERCUT BETWEEN THE TWO LOCATIONS:

David is suited, at the wheel of his car, parked up in a side
street.

                    DAVID:
               (calmly, on his mobile)
          I just wanted to share my
          commiserations about your Mum. With
          her having to have chemo all over
          again.

Grant's expression suddenly turns sour.

                    DAVID: (CONT'D)
               (on his mobile)
          I hope there's something that can
          be done for her - maybe another
          operation? Failing that, respite
          care?

                    GRANT:
               (exploding, on his mobile)
          How the hell do you know about my
          Mum? Leave her out of it, she's too
          sick to defend herself -

Ellie leans forward, concerned.

                    GRANT: (CONT'D)
               (yelling, on his mobile)
          Leave me alone, leave my Mum alone
          and -

Ellie reaches across to Grant, takes the phone from him and
silently cuts the call.

Grant has turned pale underneath his tan.

                    ELLIE:
          What happened?

                    GRANT:
          David must have hacked into my
          private emails. He was going on
          about my Mumm's chemo. How else
          would he know that?

Ellie looks horrified.

                    ELLIE:
          Oh, God. I'm so sorry. I feel
          terrible after what you did for me -

                    GRANT:
          Don't be. But Jesus, what a freak!
          I could frickin' throttle him -

                    ELLIE:
          Don't go there, Grant -

                    GRANT:
          Of course I won't. I don't know
          what he'd do to me -

Ellie bursts into tears.

                    GRANT: (CONT'D)
          Hey, sweetheart. Come here.

They hold each other tightly as she weeps. Grant wipes tears
away from his eyes.

                    GRANT: (CONT'D)
          We'll get through this, OK?
          Together. We'll find a way.

They part temporarily, look at each other. Slowly, Ellie
leans in towards Grant, and kisses him.

The screech of tyres as a car suddenly accelerates past them.
Ellie pulls back from Grant, terrified.

                    ELLIE:
          That was him!!

Ellie and Grant share horrified looks.

                                        CUT TO:

SC 87. EXT. NORTH END ROAD. FULHAM. LONDON. EVENING.

Ellie is hurrying, head down, along North End Road with a
supermarket bag of food. She bumps into Sam. The two hug, and
then Sam takes a step back.

                         SAM:
          Oh my God. You've lost tons of
          weight.

                         ELLIE:
          Yeah - lots going on. Don't worry,
          I'm still eating loads -

                         SAM:
          You still deep in work?

                         ELLIE:
          Yeah, I've just - had my head down.

                         SAM:
          I miss you. Why don't we have one
          of our catch ups?

Ellie hesitates.

                         ELLIE:
          There's so much going on right now -

                         SAM:
          Come on. Let's meet up tomorrow
          night for a drink, and you can fill
          me in -

A split second's hesitation from Ellie.

                         ELLIE:
          K.

                                        CUT TO:

SC 88. EXT. MANSION FLAT. FULHAM. LONDON. DAY.

Looking jumpy, Ellie goes back to her flat. As she puts the
key in the communal front door, she looks all around her and
behind her fearfully.

No sign of David.

                                        CUT TO:

SC 89. INT. BATHROOM. ELLIE'S FLAT. FULHAM. LONDON. NIGHT.

Ellie faces her wan, exhausted reflection in the bathroom
mirror. She puts on her make-up slowly, brushes her hair.

Changes into a purple mini-dress. Looks at her reflection
again.

Suddenly, a lava-like rage boils up out of her. She yells, a full-bodied yell from her gut, hurls her hairbrush at the mirror, which cracks.

Ellie digs her fists in her eyes, cries tears of hate. For David. For everything he's put her through.

                                                    CUT TO:

SC 90. INT. COCKTAIL BAR. FULHAM. LONDON. NIGHT.

Sam sitting expectantly in Kona Kai, the Polynesian-themed bar.

A large cocktail in front of her.

                                                    CUT TO:

SC 91. INT. LIVING ROOM. ELLIE'S FLAT. FULHAM. LONDON. NIGHT.

Ellie, back in stained trackie bottoms and a baggy jumper. Face red from crying. She takes a swig from an open bottle of wine on the coffee table in her living room.

                                                    CUT TO:

SC 92. INT. BEDROOM. ELLIE'S FLAT. FULHAM. LONDON. NIGHT.

Ellie walks unsteadily back into her bedroom.

                                                    CUT TO:

SC 93. INT. COCKTAIL BAR. FULHAM. LONDON. NIGHT.

The barman offers Sam a fake garland of flowers to put round her neck. Sam shrugs: 'What the hell', and accepts the garland.

                                                    CUT TO:

SC 94. INT. BEDROOM. ELLIE'S FLAT. FULHAM. LONDON. NIGHT.

Ellie collapses on her bed. She starts composing a text to Sam: 'Really sorry to do this to you but - '

Buries her head in her hands.

Then makes a decision. She grabs her laptop, composes an email with the subject line: **'Warning: I'm being stalked by my ex'** and starts to add in names of friends and colleagues into the address bar. When she's finished, there are over 250 email addresses.

She stares, transfixed, horrified at the list.

The lava-like rage boils up again. She gives a guttural yell at the screen. The cumulative effect of all of David's threats has paralysed her.

                                                        CUT TO:

SC 95. INT. COCKTAIL BAR. FULHAM. LONDON. NIGHT.

Sam takes a glug of her drink, composes a text to Ellie: 'Babe, where are you?? If you're not here in 10 mins, I'm jumping in a cab and hauling you out of your flat x'.

She looks fed up.

                                                        CUT TO:

SC 96. INT. BEDROOM. ELLIE'S FLAT. FULHAM. LONDON. NIGHT.

The wind blows her curtains in from her open window. Ellie rouses herself to shut the window.

She notices something odd outside, pushes the window up further.

The words 'Filthy whore!!' have been written in white sloping capitals on the red brick wall inside Ellie's small back garden, which is overlooked on all sides by other terraced houses.

Ellie sits back down again on her bed, shaking. Sam's text arrives. Ellie reads it, doesn't react.

                                                        CUT TO:

SC 97. EXT. BAR. FULHAM. LONDON. NIGHT.

Sam, a little tipsy and sad, and still wearing her garland, pours herself into a cab outside the bar.

                                                        CUT TO:

SC 98. INT. HALL. ELLIE'S FLAT. FULHAM. LONDON. NIGHT.

Her buzzer goes. Ellie hesitates, but the buzzer won't stop.

Ellie peers at the camera, Sam is leaning against the
communal front door.

Ellie buzzes her in, then slowly opens the door to her.

>   SAM:
>   (drunk and angry)
>   What the fuck happened to you? You
>   stood me up!!

>   ELLIE:
>   S-sorry, I just couldn't leave -

>   SAM:
>   Why not??

>   ELLIE:
>   David's threatening me. Come and
>   see -

>   CUT TO:

SC 99. INT. BEDROOM. ELLIE'S FLAT. FULHAM. LONDON. NIGHT.

Ellie shows Sam the view of 'Filthy whore' on her garden
wall.

>   SAM:
>   What?? I don't understand. Why
>   would David do this to you?

>   ELLIE:
>   Sam, he's been stalking me ever
>   since I finished with him.

Sam takes a step back.

>   SAM:
>   No way!

>   ELLIE:
>   Yep.

>   SAM:
>   Ellie, you must go to the police -

>   ELLIE:
>   (hurriedly)
>   Yeah, yeah. I have.

                         SAM:
          What are they doing about it?

                         ELLIE:
          Err, not much.

                         SAM:
          Because if you want me to go down
          there myself and re-report him
          right now, and wait with you until
          you're seen, I will do that. [beat]
          You want me to research 'stalking'
          for you? There must be things you
          can do -

                         ELLIE:
          It's fine, darling. I've got this.

[PAUSE]

Sam's not convinced.

                         SAM:
          I feel like you're shutting me out.
          Let me help you -

Ellie loses it.

                         ELLIE:
          I'm not shutting you out of
          anything, Sam! I'm just trying to
          keep it all together while this
          fucking lunatic is making my life
          really fucking hard!!

                         SAM:
          I'm so sorry, I had no idea -

                         ELLIE:
               (Bitter)
          Yeah, the fuck-up of your friend
          with the appalling taste in men.
          This probably looks like great
          entertainment for someone happily
          married.

Sam stares.

                         SAM:
          What's that got to do with it?? I
          just want you to be happy. [beat]

Sam blinks back tears.

                    SAM: (CONT'D (CONT'D)
          And I try and support you, I try
          and be here for you, and you just
          push me away.

                    ELLIE:
            (snaps)
          Oh, spare me the violins, Sam. I
          can't deal with your neediness
          right now.

                    SAM:
          Neediness?! Go fuck yourself!!

The two friends eye ball each other, furious.

                    ELLIE:
          Just go. OK?

                    SAM:
            (in tears)
          Fine.

She leaves, slamming the door after her.

Ellie curls up on the bed, still dressed. Utterly drained.
Falls sound asleep with the light still on.

                                        CUT TO:

SC 100. EXT. MANSION FLAT. FULHAM. LONDON. DAY.

Ellie cautiously opens her front door and peers out to check
the coast is clear. She's wearing baggy jeans and a hoodie
covering her face. She's carrying a washing up bowl with
soapy water and a brush.

She steps out to open her side gate and walk round to the
back garden:

                    MR P:
          Oh, I barely recognise you these
          days.

Ellie gives an almighty jump. She gives him a cursory nod,
and runs through her side gate.

Mr P shakes his head at her.

                                        CUT TO:

SC 101. EXT. ELLIE'S BACK GARDEN. FULHAM. LONDON. DAY.

Ellie sets to, manically scrubbing away at the 'Filthy whore' message on her wall.

But getting rid of the message is harder than she thought. Sweat drips off her and she's grunting with the effort.

She takes a few steps back to assess. She's succeeded in rubbing out the first three letters of 'Filthy' and nibbled away at the 'e' of 'whore'. Currently the message reads: 'Thy whor'.

>   ELLIE:
>   (To herself)
>   Frigging Shakespeare. That's all I
>   need -

She bursts out into hysterical giggles as she continues to scrub away at the message.

>   CUT TO:

SC 102. INT. LIVING ROOM. ELLIE'S FLAT. FULHAM. LONDON. DAY.

Ellie dials David's number; it goes to voice mail.

>   ELLIE:
>   (spits into her mobile)
>   I've had enough of your madness,
>   David. Stop it now, or I'm going to
>   the police -

>   CUT TO:

SC 103. INT. KITCHEN. ELLIE'S FLAT. FULHAM. LONDON. DAY.

Ellie dumps down a bottle of wine on her kitchen table, with a huge bag of crisps.

>   CUT TO:

SC 104. INT. LIVING ROOM. ELLIE'S FLAT. FULHAM. LONDON. DAY.

Ellie sits on her sofa, swigging from the bottle and cramming her mouth with crisps - like a hungry animal. She looks utterly defeated.

>   CUT TO:

SC 105. INT. BATHROOM. ELLIE'S FLAT. FULHAM. LONDON. DAY.

The morning after the night before. Ellie wearily faces
herself in the bath room mirror, attempts to cover up last
night's damage with make-up.

A smart knock on her door.

                                                    CUT TO:

SC 106. INT HALL. ELLIE'S FLAT. FULHAM. LONDON. DAY.

Ellie looks through the spy hole, and opens the door to see a
couple of uniformed PC's [one male, one female, 30's] on the
landing.

                    PC DUDLEY:
          Ellie Somerville? Your ex partner,
          David Swithins, has filed a
          complaint against you for harassing
          him and his family on his property.
          Would you come with us now to the
          station for questioning?

Ellie rocks back in horror.

                    ELLIE:
          I'm just about to leave for work.

                    WPC LAINES:
          Sorry about that. But we need you
          down the station.

                    ELLIE:
          But he's the one harassing me!?

                    DUDLEY:
          Have you filed a report with the
          police?

                    ELLIE:
          Err ... not yet. My job's very
          busy.

The two coppers exchange looks.

                    LAINES:
          If you don't come voluntarily,
          Ellie, we will have to arrest you.

                    ELLIE:
          Jesus.

Ellie grabs her denim jacket, work bag and mobile.

                                        CUT TO:

SC 107. EXT. MANSION FLAT. FULHAM. LONDON. DAY.

Ellie frantically calls Grant on her mobile, gets his voice
mail.

                    ELLIE:
               (on her mobile)
          Grant, the police have just turned
          up. I've got to down the station
          for questioning. Because - guess
          what - David has reported me for
          harassing him!! So sorry, I know
          we've got a client meeting. I'll be
          in as soon as I can.

She gets into the back of the police squad car.

                                        CUT TO:

SC 108. INT. GRANT'S OFFICE. ZEBRA HQ. EUSTON ROAD. LONDON.
DAY.

Grant's mobile rings out on his desk. The office is deserted.

                                        CUT TO:

SC 109. INT. CONFERENCE ROOM TWO. ZEBRA HQ. EUSTON ROAD.
LONDON. DAY.

Grant and the client, Louise, sit in uncomfortable silence.
Waiting.

                    LOUISE:
          Is she running late or would she
          have forgotten??

                    GRANT:
          I can only apologise, Louise. She
          doesn't normally do this. I'll run
          through what she's written for you
          to date. Then we can go from there.

Louise nods, clearly not happy.

                                        CUT TO:

SC 110. INT. POLICE INTERVIEW ROOM. POLICE STATION.
HAMMERSMITH. LONDON. DAY.

A nondescript room, with dirty scuff marks and dents in the
white painted walls.

The door opens, Ellie looks round.

In walks **DCI RENSHAW** [40's, bald, tough nut] and **DC PATEL**
[30's, put upon].

Renshaw leans across the table at Ellie, who looks at him
doubtfully.

>   RENSHAW;
>   So, this isn't looking good from
>   your point of view, Ellie, and I
>   strongly advise you to get a
>   lawyer. A professional woman like
>   you, accused of harassing her ex
>   partner.

>   ELLIE:
>   No, it wasn't like that. Why on
>   earth do I need a lawyer? I've done
>   nothing wrong.

Renshaw and Patel exchange looks.

>   RENSHAW:
>   Here's how it's stacking up. David
>   has already made a statement to the
>   police -

Ellie raises an eyebrow at this.

>   RENSHAW: (CONT'D)
>   Yep - he's stated that you have a
>   history of abusive relationships
>   that have left you paranoid and
>   suspicious.

>   ELLIE:
>   I had one abusive relationship with
>   a guy called Karl - but what the
>   hell?!

>   RENSHAW:
>   And that despite you giving David
>   keys to your flat early on in your
>   relationship, you tried to get into
>   David's phone when you were
>   together as you were constantly
>   mistrustful of his intentions.

                    ELLIE:
          It wasn't like that! He asked me
          for the keys. I said I wasn't
          ready, it was too early, something
          like that.

                    RENSHAW:
          But you gave them to him anyway.

                    ELLIE:
          No. I tried to say that it was too
          soon. Then David asked me if I
          didn't think we were getting on. I
          said we were, and then he kissed
          me.

          He must have taken that as
          confirmation to copy the keys.

          But I didn't even know he had my
          keys until he let some removal guys
          into my flat to take away the
          fridge he bought me!!

Renshaw jots down notes. Then moves in for the kill again.

                    RENSHAW:
          Would you say you're a heavy
          drinker, Ellie?

Ellie freezes.

                    ELLIE:
          I like a drink, now and then.

                    RENSHAW:
          Now and then? Every day? Every
          night? Once, twice? How many units
          a week?

Ellie falls silent.

                    RENSHAW: (CONT'D)
          David's statement mentions heavy
          drinking which only added to an
          already volatile relationship.

                    ELLIE:
          What are you talking about??

                    RENSHAW:
          Threatening him under the
          influence, sending abusive text
          messages, hoping he'll get hit by a
          bus. For example.

                    ELLIE:
          That was because he turned up at my
          work a few days after I chucked
          him, pretending we had a business
          meeting. He wanted to intimidate
          and humiliate me -

                    RENSHAW:
          Yeah, he said that it was just a
          business meeting. He has meetings
          all over town, apparently.

          How do you explain following him to
          his house, making a scene in front
          of his wife and kid, accusing him
          of having an affair to his wife -
          who is now being treated for
          depression and anxiety? And who, by
          the way, is willing to give us a
          Witness Statement.

                    ELLIE:
          He lied to me about his marriage!
          He told me they were getting a
          divorce when they were still living
          under the same roof!!

Renshaw eyes Ellie coolly.

                    RENSHAW:
          Since then, David's wife has kicked
          him out of the family home. He's
          brought this complaint against you
          so he can defend himself against a
          woman who he thinks is mentally
          unstable.

Ellie stares at Renshaw in horror. How has it come to this?

She feels the lava-like rage rise up in her again.

                    ELLIE:
          You've got it all wrong. David
          pursued me for a relationship,
          misled me about being available.
          And when I ended it, he started
          harassing me, my colleagues, my Mum
          and Dad.

Something in Renshaw's expression changes. Patel shifts uneasily in her chair.

Ellie senses this, and presses her advantage.

                    ELLIE: (CONT'D)
          He's waged a campaign against me,
          turning up at the same pub where my
          work colleague, Grant, and I were
          having lunch -

                    RENSHAW:
          Yeah, he said you'd say that.
          Apparently he frequents that pub
          himself after visiting a certain
          client in town.

Ellie rolls her eyes.

                    ELLIE:
          Can't you see he's playing you?

Renshaw turns round his laptop and plays a few seconds of CCTV footage with Grant shouting at David, who is sitting down, calmly.

                    RENSHAW:
          So you sleep with this guy, David,
          make him fall for you. Then you
          accuse him of all sorts, ruin his
          marriage. And then you use Grant to
          do your dirty work for you.

                    ELLIE:
          No! Grant insisted on going over
          there himself!

                    RENSHAW:
          And pursued a sexual relationship
          with Grant, who is clearly the
          aggressor with David -

                    ELLIE:
          My private life after David has got
          nothing to do with this.

Renshaw looks at Ellie balefully.

                    ELLIE: (CONT'D)
          David then came to the leaving do
          for Lucy, our receptionist at work.
          He sat at the opposite end of the
          bar as me!

                    RENSHAW:
          What David chooses to do after
          hours is none of your business.

Ellie frowns.

                    RENSHAW: (CONT'D)
          Or were you jealous that he'd moved
          onto someone else?

                    ELLIE:
          No, of course not! You're
          completely missing the point!

Ellie regards Renshaw with despair. She can't figure out if
he's giving her a hard time because she's a woman, or whether
Renshaw has already decided that she's guilty.

                    PATEL:
          According to David's statement, he
          made friends with Lucy on an
          earlier occasion and she invited
          him along to her leaving do.

                    ELLIE:
          He turned up unannounced at my
          parents' B&B. He even jumped onto
          our video call.

Finally: Renshaw's expression falters. Patel looks pointedly
at her boss.

                    RENSHAW:
          Yeah, he did say that he had
          previously booked a stay at your
          parents' B&B. After his wife kicked
          him out, he had nowhere else to go.
          But he realizes in retrospect it
          was wrong to go there.

                    PATEL:
          Do you have any evidence of your
          claims against him?

Ellie picks up her mobile to go through it, and then
remembers her drunken purge the other night.

                    ELLIE:
          Oh, shit. I deleted all his texts
          and messages from my phone.

Renshaw rolls his eyes.

                    ELLIE: (CONT'D)
          And he wrote 'Filthy whore' on my
          garden wall the other night - but I
          scrubbed most of it off.

                    PATEL:
          When was this, Ellie, that you got
          rid of the messages?

Ellie looks up. Patel's voice is soft. She senses a kindred
spirit.

                    ELLIE:
          About a week ago. It was after he
          jumped on the video call with my
          Mum and Dad. I was so fed up with
          it all and - decided to get rid of
          everything he's ever sent or done
          to me.

Renshaw's eyes close momentarily. He suddenly looks very
tired.

                    ELLIE: (CONT'D)
          Can't you guys trace what he sent
          me? Find it in the trash can on my
          phone, or something?

                    PATEL:
          We'd have to ask our Forensics
          colleagues to have a thorough look,
          see what they can recover -

                    RENSHAW:
          We'll be in touch if we find
          anything. In the meantime, stay
          away from David.

                    ELLIE:
          As if I'd go anywhere near him.

                    RENSHAW;
          And do yourself a favour. Get a
          lawyer.

Reeling, confused, Ellie hands over her mobile.

                    PATEL:
          In case you find any more evidence
          of potential stalking, here's the
          card of our colleague, Donna
          Carter. She works in the Witness
          Care Unit here.

Ellie nods. Puts the card in her pocket.

CUT TO:

SC 111. INT. GRANT'S OFFICE. ZEBRA OFFICES. EUSTON ROAD.
LONDON. DAY.

Wearily, Ellie walks in.

Grant looks at the clock on the wall: it's 12.45 pm.

> GRANT:
> You missed our Quarterly Business
> Review with Louise.

> ELLIE:
> (hisses)
> I called you, left a voice mail. I
> got arrested this morning because
> David's accused me of stalking him -

Grant stares at Ellie, anger slowly draining away to make way
for concern.

> GRANT:
> Oh man. I left my phone in my
> office during my client meeting.
> I'm so sorry. Are you OK?

> ELLIE:
> (sarcastic)
> Yeah. Never better. [beat] Of
> course I'm not OK, Grant! They gave
> me hell. And I've been such an
> idiot. Last week I got rid of all
> his texts and videos on my phone -

> GRANT:
> The evidence -

> ELLIE:
> Yeah. They even showed me CCTV
> footage of you threatening David in
> the pub -

Grant looks at her, alarmed.

> GRANT:
> I think you should take a step back
> from work for a while, with
> everything going on. Tell HR you're
> being stalked.
> (MORE)

                    GRANT: (CONT'D)
          I could try and explain to Louise
          what's going on, though you know
          how uptight she is -

                    ELLIE:
          No! Work means everything to me,
          you know that - I don't want Louise
          or HR knowing about my private life
          -

                    GRANT:
          Hey, I get it. And I'm really
          rooting for you. But -

                    ELLIE:
          What? I thought we were in this
          together.

Ellie moves closer to Grant. And closer still. He can sense
her desperation.

                    ELLIE: (CONT'D)
          Please Grant. I thought we were a -
          a - unit - that we could beat the
          bastard together.

Grant looks wretched: wresting with his conflicting
loyalties, to serve his client and ultimately keep his job,
while risking a burgeoning relationship with Ellie.

                    GRANT:
          We are in this together but - look,
          this is really difficult.

                    ELLIE:
          It's not exactly easy for me!! Are
          you saying you don't want to help?

                    GRANT:
          No, babe. I want to support you - .
          But you're not going to like this.
          [beat] Louise's removed you from
          the SnackSnack account. With
          immediate effect.

                    ELLIE:
          What?? No!

                    GRANT:
          She's questioned your commitment.

                    ELLIE:
          You know there's reasons for this.
          I'm totally committed!

Grant looks apologetic.

                    GRANT:
          Sorry. My hands are kinda tied. I
          don't want us to lose the entire
          account -

Ellie's eyes fill with tears. Grant clocks how vulnerable she
looks.

                    GRANT: (CONT'D)
               (guilty)
          I'm so sorry, Ellie. But unless you
          tell Louise what's going on, her
          mind's made up.

Ellie shakes her head.

                    GRANT: (CONT'D)
          In that case, take a few days off,
          get some sleep. And in the
          meantime, I'll ask around - see if
          we can move you onto another
          consumer account.

                    ELLIE:
          Grant, am I being fired??

                    GRANT:
          No, you're just - between accounts.

Ellie gets up abruptly, leaves.

Grant stares after her, helplessly.

                                        CUT TO:

SC 112. INT. ELLIE'S KITCHEN. ELLIE'S FLAT. LONDON. DAY.

Ellie peers gloomily inside her small, unremarkable-looking
fridge, bought to replace the expensive model. She finds a
hunk of cheese, takes it out and gnaws at it.

Staring at the photos of happier times on the outside door.
Something in one photo makes her look closer. She takes the
picture off, and studies it.

                    ELLIE:
          Oh my God.

There's her and Sam, snapped at a Christmas party in a bar
two years ago. Inches away from her, staring intently at her,
is David. Standing alone at the bar, drink in his hand.

Feverishly, she scans the other photos, finds something else.

This time, 13 months ago. A selfie of her and Sam outside the
Zebra offices, Ellie brandishing a champagne bottle to
celebrate her promotion onto the SnackSnack account. Leaning
against a bus stop opposite them ... is David. Hands in
pockets. Watching her.

Ellie rocks back, holding the photos. Shocked, terrified.

She staggers to her breakfast bar, where she left Donna
Carter's business card, and rings the number.

                                        CUT TO:

SC 113. INT. OFFICE. WITNESS CARE UNIT. HAMMERSMITH. LONDON.
NIGHT.

WPC DONNA CARTER [40's, mixed race, big hair] eases herself
into a hard-backed wooden chair opposite Ellie. Her manner is
light and casual, but she has the air of a big cat, waiting
to pounce.

                    DONNA:
            What have you got?

                    ELLIE:
            I found him in two photos taken up
            to two years ago. I didn't even
            know him then -

Donna leans forward.

                    DONNA:
            Show me -

                    ELLIE:
            That one was taken at a Christmas
            party. Some bar in Fulham -

                    DONNA:
            Can you remember which one?

Ellie screws up her face, remembering.

                    ELLIE:
            Evans & Peel, Detective Agency.

Donna raises an incredulous eyebrow.

                    ELLIE: (CONT'D)
          It's a speakeasy bar, themed as a
          Prohibition -

                    DONNA:
          Right. Did you talk to him at all
          that night?

                    ELLIE:
          No. I never even noticed him.

                    DONNA:
          Interesting. And this one?

                    ELLIE:
          This was 13 months ago. I'm with my
          friend, Sam outside my offices. And
          there he is -

                    DONNA:
          Outside your workplace. Hhm.

                    ELLIE:
          They're proof, right?

                    DONNA:
          This is definitely evidence of him
          stalking you, following you for the
          past two years before you even knew
          him. You can see he's looking at
          you in the photos.

Ellie nods.

                    ELLIE:
          Yeah, and I turn round in shops,
          he's there. He's in bars around
          London. Wherever I go. Or went.
          [beat] I've stopped having a social
          life.

                    DONNA:
              (scribbling notes)
          I'll ask my colleagues in Forensics
          to see if he's put a GPS tracker on
          your phone.

                    ELLIE:
          Wh-what?

                    DONNA:
          You've brought your laptop with
          you? Good. Let's have a look at
          that.

She checks Ellie's personal laptop.

> DONNA: (CONT'D)
> Nothing on here either. Turn out
> your pockets, would you?

Ellie places a mound of keys, chewing gum and hair grips on
the table. Donna sifts through the pile and lifts out a
tracking device with a crooked finger.

> ELLIE:
> What's that?

> DONNA:
> If you lose your keys it can find
> them for you. But David's obviously
> been using it to track your
> movements. Didn't you get any
> alerts from your mobile about an
> 'unknown accessory'?

Ellie's face falls.

> ELLIE:
> Oh God, yes, a couple of times. I
> just deleted them because David
> said it was a stupid error message
> for something. Sorry, not very
> technical.

Donna raises a sceptical eyebrow.

> DONNA:
> You need to take yourself seriously
> and be vigilant, Ellie. This guy's
> on your case. And it looks as if
> it's been a couple of years. You
> need to be on your case to get him
> off yours. Got it?

Ellie nods, chastened.

> DONNA: (CONT'D)
> Tell your friends and family to
> check their belongings, because
> it's possible he's put trackers on
> them too.

Ellie's eyes widen with a realisation.

> ELLIE:
> He's let himself into my flat
> several times without my even -
> knowing.
> (MORE)

                    ELLIE: (CONT'D)
          He opened my window, moved the
          keys, and left a cup of tea out on
          a coffee table when he knows I
          normally wash it and put it upside
          down on the draining board. Small
          changes like that, to mess with my
          head -

Donna nods.

                    DONNA:
          So here's what you do from now on.
          Keep a record of everything that
          happens. Do NOT engage with him or
          approach him. Change your routines,
          your routes to work. Change your
          mobile number -

                    ELLIE:
                (spits back)
          No, not doing that. I've got
          hundreds of work contacts in my
          phone.

Donna spreads her palms.

                    DONNA:
          Fine. Get yourself a different
          phone anyway. And come off social
          media.

[PAUSE]

Ellie nods.

                    DONNA: (CONT'D)
          I recommend you install CCTV in or
          outside your flat, if possible.
          Keep an overnight bag packed with
          essentials if you need to leave
          home in a hurry.

Ellie's face tightens with fear. Donna sees this, leans
across and squeezes Ellie's hand.

                    DONNA: (CONT'D)
          We'll get the ball rolling, OK?
          I'll get David arrested for
          harassment. Because at the very
          least, he qualifies for a Warning.

Donna watches Ellie carefully. Ellie looks like she's processing a lot of information, coming to grips with her reality: that David is stalking her, and there are actions that can be taken.

> DONNA: (CONT'D)
> (treading carefully)
> I don't want to alarm you. But you'll probably have to take David to court to get a Restraining Order. Otherwise he won't stop. A Harassment Warning is like a slap on the wrist to a man like him -

> ELLIE:
> Oh, no. I can't do that. What about the damage to my reputation? He'll ruin me -

> DONNA:
> No he won't, Ellie. I reckon you're strong enough to face him off in court. [beat] Think about it, and come back to me with your decision.

Depressed by this turn of events, Ellie nods.

> CUT TO:

SC 114. EXT. OUTSIDE WITNESS CARE UNIT. HAMMERSMITH. LONDON. NIGHT.

Ellie checks up and down the street for David. No sign of him.

She walks to a bus stop, shivering, and waits for the bus.

> CUT TO:

SC 115. EXT. MANSION FLAT. FULHAM. LONDON. NIGHT.

Ellie checks her watch as she slowly approaches her block of flats: 9.31 pm.

She stops dead. David is waiting for her at her gate, arms folded. She approaches him, fury overcoming fear.

> ELLIE:
> What the hell do you want?

David is unshaven, dressed in jeans and a stained sweatshirt,
baseball cap pulled low on his head. He looks and smells as
if he hasn't washed for a week.

> DAVID:
> Just to talk, Ellie. I wanna work
> things out -

> ELLIE:
> There's nothing to work out, David.
> We're over. Leave me alone.

Ellie pushes past David to get to her front door, but David
grabs her by the left arm, holds her fast. She can smell the
alcohol on his breath.

> DAVID:
> Because of you, Nathalie's back on
> the happy pills. Forbidden me to
> see Benny, and I'm sleeping in my
> car. It's all gone to shit -

> ELLIE:
> I'm sorry, but it's not my fault,
> David. You lied to me about
> everything.

> DAVID:
> You led me on, you little whore!
> Thanks to you, the police came to
> my office today to give me a
> Warning. And to cap it all, now
> Nathalie wants a divorce. You've
> destroyed me!

Ellie scrambles to get free of David, he holds onto her
tighter, and she pushes him back. The lava-like rage boils up
and out of her.

> ELLIE:
> (yelling)
> I hate you! Fucking leave me
> alone!!

As they fight, Ellie reaches into her pocket and brings out
her flat keys balled into her fist and slams them, hard,
against David's throat.

David staggers back, clutching his throat. Ellie runs back
down her road, gasping with fear.

> CUT TO:

SC 116. EXT. NORTH END ROAD. FULHAM. LONDON. NIGHT.

Ellie looks round wildly. She uses her new pay-as-you-go
mobile to dial Grant, who picks up immediately.

>   GRANT:
>   (VO)
>   Hello?

>   ELLIE:
>   (stuttering, on her
>   mobile)
>   I can't, I can't go home. David's
>   outside - he's outside -

>   GRANT:
>   (VO)
>   Jump in a cab, come to mine.

>   ELLIE:
>   (on her mobile)
>   You, you sure?

>   GRANT:
>   (VO)
>   Do it now.

>   CUT TO:

SC 117. EXT. ROAD. FULHAM. LONDON. NIGHT.

Ellie rings the door bell to a smart-looking town house in a
quiet residential street choked with cars.

She looks shy and overwhelmed.

Grant opens the door, wearing a novelty t'shirt, boxer shorts
and fluffy rabbit slippers.

Ellie can't resist a joke.

>   ELLIE:
>   It's a good look -

>   GRANT:
>   My athleisure wear. Let's get you
>   inside.

>   CUT TO:

SC 118. INT. GRANT'S LIVING ROOM. GRANT'S FLAT. ROAD. FULHAM. LONDON. NIGHT.

Ellie anxiously sits on the edge of his sofa, Grant next to her.

> ELLIE:
> (on her mobile)
> Yeah, I want to leave an urgent
> message for Donna Carter of the
> Witness Care Unit. I reported my ex
> partner, David, for stalking me
> this evening, along with my family
> and colleagues. He was waiting for
> me outside my flat this evening and
> we had - he was violent -

Grant sits nearer Ellie on hearing this.

> DUTY OFFICER:
> (VO)
> Where are you now?

> ELLIE:
> (on her mobile)
> At a friend's house.

There's a loud, insistent hammering on the door. Ellie and Grant look at each other.

> GRANT:
> It's 11.40 at night, for fuck's
> sake.

Ellie ducks down, still on her mobile. She peers out of the blinds and sees David glancing appraisingly at Grant's house from the front door.

Ellie crouches right down, terrified.

> ELLIE:
> (on her mobile)
> He's outside!

David starts banging again on the front door.

> DAVID:
> (shouts)
> Let me in!!

Grant leaps up.

> GRANT:
> I'm going to tell him to -

Ellie hangs onto Grant for dear life. They tussle.

>ELLIE:
>(on her mobile)
>No, Grant. Please don't -

>GRANT:
>No, I'm fed up of this. Somebody
>has to do something if the cops are
>dragging their feet -

>ELLIE:
>(frantic, on her mobile)
>11a Mortimer Gardens, Fulham.

>DUTY OFFICER:
>(VO)
>Don't answer the door to him.

The sound of breaking glass. Ellie and Grant pause, look at each other.

David bursts in through the smashed living room window.

Grant runs towards him but David head butts him.

>ELLIE:
>(on her mobile)
>Stop it, David!

>GRANT:
>Ahh. Fuck -

Grant falls to the floor, clutching his nose, which is bleeding heavily.

>DAVID:
>I wish I'd never wasted my life on
>you!

>>CUT TO:

SC 119. EXT. HAMMERSMITH BROADWAY. LONDON. NIGHT.

A police patrol car speeds down, siren on.

>>CUT TO:

SC 120. INT. LIVING ROOM. GRANT'S FLAT. FULHAM. LONDON. NIGHT.

Ellie holds David in her gaze.

                         ELLIE:
                    (tentative)
               Maybe it's a good thing that
               Nathalie's divorcing you. If it's
               over between you, like you say -

David flares up instantly.

                         DAVID:
               Look, I've had loads of women in my
               marriage, right from the get go.
               But none got under my skin like you
               have, Ellie. It's not too late for
               us. I'll never stop loving you.
               Even though you've hurt me so much.

                         ELLIE:
               I'm so sorry for hurting you, and
               upsetting Nathalie. But it's over
               between you and me now. Can't you
               just leave me and my friends alone?
               Please, David -

David looks at her and Grant, who is lying winded on the
floor, dabbing at his nose with his wrist.

                         DAVID:
               Are you sleeping together?

                         ELLIE:
               No -

                         DAVID:
               Fucking liar -

David suddenly lunges at Ellie, puts his arm around Ellie's
neck. From his pocket he produces a Stanley knife which he
presses against her jugular.

He starts dragging Ellie from the room.

                         ELLIE:
               David, stop - !

                                                  CUT TO:

SC 121. INT HALL. GRANT'S FLAT. FULHAM. LONDON. NIGHT.

Ellie struggles against David's hold, but he's stronger and
hauls her across the threshold.

ELLIE:
Please, let me go -

SC 122. EXT. GARDEN PATH. GRANT'S FLAT. FULHAM. LONDON.
NIGHT.

Grant blunders out, blocking David's progress down the path.
His nose looks bloody.

GRANT:
There's nothing to worry about.
We're just work mates -

DAVID:
(yells)
And you're a fucking liar, too!! I
saw you kiss her -

Grant hurls himself at David, punches him hard in the face.
David staggers back, letting go of Ellie.

Grant rains several blows on David. In the confusion, David
stabs Grant in the breast bone, who drops down onto the path,
bleeding.

ELLIE:
(screams)
Grant, no!

But Ellie can't get near Grant because David's threatening
her with the Stanley knife.

A police patrol car screeches to a halt outside the gate and
PC Dudley and WPC Laines sprint towards the group.

ELLIE: (CONT'D)
(points)
Grant's been stabbed -

Dudley applies pressure to Grant's stab wound while speaking
into his radio.

DUDLEY:
01FH to Control. Send ambulance and
urgent back-up. One IC1 male
stabbed. Over.

Dudley's radio crackles in reply.

Laines walks towards David with her palms up, but David
doesn't budge.

                    LAINES:
          David, drop the knife.

                    DAVID:
          Go to hell -

                    LAINES:
          Look, if you drop the knife, we can
          talk things over. Calmly.

                    DAVID:
          I'm done with cosy chats.

                    LAINES:
          You've already hurt one person. I
          don't believe you really want to
          hurt Ellie, do you? Because I know
          you love her.

David's eyes fill with tears.

                    DAVID:
          All of this mess is because I love
          her. And I think she loves me too.
          But she's a complete and utter
          whore, a bitch, and she's fucked me
          over, big time -

Laines swaps a look with Ellie, who takes an invisible cue
from her.

                    ELLIE:
          You're right. I do still love you,
          David, but I'm scared - scared to
          commit -

                    DAVID:
          I know, it takes a long time to let
          love in. It took me two years to
          pluck up the courage to talk to
          you.

                    ELLIE:
          Why?

David takes a deep breath.

                    DAVID:
          Because you intimidate me, Ellie.

Ellie rocks back, confounded by this admission.

Laines takes a few more steps towards David, palms still outstretched.

                    LAINES:
          Put the knife down, David. If you
          stop now, we can just go down the
          station and talk it over. Sort
          things out. But if you carry on,
          things could get even messier -

                    DAVID:
          Meaning?

                    LAINES:
          Put it like this. If you harm a
          hair of Ellie's head, you'll be
          spending an even longer time banged
          up.

David studies Laines carefully. Something in what she's said has obviously landed with him. Then slowly he drops the knife. It falls with a clatter onto the garden path.

Dudley and Laines smartly turn David round and cuff him with his hands behind his back.

                    LAINES: (CONT'D)
          David Swithins, I'm arresting you
          on suspicion of stalking of Ellie
          Somerville and possession of an
          offensive weapon. You do not have
          to say anything. But it may harm
          your defence if you do not mention
          when questioned something which you
          later rely on in court -

Ellie staggers towards Grant, who's been attended to by a paramedic on a trolley beside a waiting ambulance.

LATER:

Grant, attached to a drip, is wheeled into an ambulance on a stretcher. Ellie clambers in after him.

David watches them morosely from the back of a patrol car.

One of two **PARAMEDICS** [male, 40's] shuts the doors while the other monitors Grant.

                                        CUT TO:

SC 123. INT. CORRIDOR. CHARING CROSS HOSPITAL. LONDON. NIGHT.

Ellie paces up and down, beside herself with anxiety. Wild-eyed, sleepless.

After a few turns up and down, she plops back down, exhausted.

Eventually, a **NURSE** [female, 50's] appears. Ellie lifts her head from off the greasy hospital wall.

>   NURSE:
> Ellie?

>   ELLIE:
> Yes, that's me.

>   NURSE:
> Grant is out of danger. He's
> stable.

>   ELLIE:
> Oh, thank God!

The nurse gives Ellie an appraising glance.

>   NURSE:
> You his next of kin?

>   ELLIE:
>   (winging it)
> Yeah.

>   NURSE:
> You can have a couple of minutes
> with him. He's heavily sedated,
> mind.

Ellie breathes out.

>   ELLIE:
> Thank you -

>   CUT TO:

SC 124. INT. WARD. CHARING CROSS HOSPITAL. LONDON. NIGHT.

Ellie is at Grant's bedside, tenderly watching over him. Then she bends over and kisses him gently on the forehead.

She turns around as she hears a cough from outside. Both Sam and Rob are peering in through the glass at her from out in the corridor. She opens the door and she and Sam fall back into the ward, and into each other's arms.

                    ELLIE:
                 (welling up)
          I'm so sorry -

                    SAM:
          I've got you.

Ellie hugs Rob.

                    ELLIE:
          Thank you for being here.

                    ROB:
          Thanks for calling.

                                        CUT TO:

SC 125. INT. COURT. LONDON. DAY.

On-screen titles: **Three months later.**

Ellie stands behind a screen, while David, his head hanging, sits in the dock opposite the screen.

Grant, Sam and Rob, her Mum and Dad are in the public gallery.

                    ELLIE:
                 (reading her Witness
                  Statement)
          Being stalked is like being under
          siege. When there's a lull, I'd
          temporarily forget about David,
          breathe a sigh of relief and carry
          on with my life. Then every time
          I'd relax, he'd be back in contact
          and it would start all over again.
          And the conflicting emotions would
          come flooding back: the terror, the
          anxiety - what's he going to do
          next? The pity, the shame, the
          disappointment. How could I not
          have seen the signs that he was
          unstable? And the sheer,
          overwhelming, gut-wrenching hatred
          of him.
                    (MORE)

ELLIE: (CONT'D)
That someone can seemingly wreck
another person's life so easily,
and that it has to get really
seriously bad before the police
intervene. Simply put, without a
permanent Restraining Order or
Protective Order, I don't know how
I'll ever get David out of my life.

CUT TO:

SC 126. INT. WAITING ROOM. COURT. LONDON. DAY.

A cramped, airless room. Ellie sits, holding hands tightly
with her Mum and Sam.

CONNIE:
Are you alright, darling?

ELLIE:
Yes, thanks. Just glad you're here.

CONNIE:
How long until the judge makes his
decision?

ELLIE:
No idea. But if Grant's giving his
evidence now, it could be hours
yet.

She seems stronger, more determined. At peace, even.

LATER:

SAM:
I almost forgot to tell you,
amongst all the excitement.

ELLIE:
What's that?

SAM:
We're expecting a baby -

Ellie squeals and hugs Sam tightly.

CONNIE:
Oh, darling. So pleased for you.

ELLIE:
You'll make a brilliant Mum.

Donna appears at the door, grinning from ear to ear. Her Dad, Rob and Grant are there, too.

>   ELLIE: (CONT'D)
>   Well??

>   DONNA:
>   You've done it. David's been given
>   a Protective Order of three years,
>   and a custodial sentence of six
>   months.

Ellie's mouth drops open.

>   ELLIE:
>   Wow. I did not expect that.

Grant approaches Ellie, beaming. In full view of everyone, he plants a kiss on her lips.

>   GRANT:
>   Well done, babes. I knew you'd do
>   it.

>   ELLIE:
>   Thank you.

They look happy and in love.

>   CUT TO:

SC 127. EXT. OUTSIDE COURT. LONDON. DAY.

Ellie, Grant, Sam and Rob, and her parents spill out onto the court steps, still excited. Donna is outside, having a sneaky ciggie.

As Ellie hops down the steps, she bumps smack into a distraught-looking Benny, and a stoney-faced Nathalie.

>   BENNY:
>   (yells)
>   I hate you! Taking my Dad away from
>   me!!

Ellie's joy is utterly punctured. Donna looks over, stubs out her cigarette.

>   ELLIE:
>   Benny, your Dad lied to me, and to
>   your Mum.

Nathalie pulls Benny away from them.

                    NATHALIE:
                 (hisses)
            You think that it was all about
            you. Believe me, you are not the
            first of his little 'friends'. I
            have always had to share my
            marriage but in its own way it
            worked. You just had to ruin it.

                    ELLIE:
            How could you make something like
            that work??

                    NATHALIE:
            God kept me strong. And I chose to
            turn the other cheek.

Ellie wheels round, gutted by the implications of this.

                    ELLIE:
            Why did you stay with him, if you
            knew what he was like??

Nathalie's face crumples. Donna creeps nearer, and nearer
towards them both.

                    NATHALIE:
            Because despite everything, I love
            him. And for me, where I'm from,
            family is everything. And in his
            way, he loves me. I guess. [beat]
            It tears me apart to say it, but he
            - loves you. I saw the way he
            looked at you. You had something
            different from all the other girls.

                    ELLIE:
            What do you mean?

                    NATHALIE:
            You were the first woman to tell
            him 'no'. In reality, it just
            worsened his obsession with you -

Ellie shudders involuntarily.

                    ELLIE:
            But you threw him out after I
            confronted him.

                    NATHALIE:
            No. Despite all that he's done. I
            would never throw him out.

                    ELLIE:
          I don't understand. David told me
          you did.

                    NATHALIE:
             (sad)
          He lied.

Ellie and Donna gaze at Nathalie in appalled disbelief.

                    ELLIE:
          Nathalie, your husband stalked me
          for two years. And I only met him
          four months ago.

Nathalie slumps back, with the glimmerings of insight into
what she enabled David to do.

Ellie and Donna share a long look with each other. Grant
approaches Ellie, holds his hand out to her.

                    END

[titles up - play out on 'Papa Was A Rollin' Stone by The
Temptations].

Printed in Great Britain
by Amazon

28605269R00059